Life, Death and Everything Else

Lynn Fesenmeyer-Johnson

Life, Death and Everything Else

Alternative Book Press
alternativebookpress.com

2024 Paperback Edition
Copyright © 2024 by Lynn Fesenmeyer-Johnson
All Rights Reserved

Cover Design by Kristin Waters

Book Design by Alternative Book Press

LIBRARY OF CONGRESS CATALOGING-IN-PUBLICATION DATA

Fesenmeyer-Johnson, Lynn / Life, Death and Everything Else/ First Edition
Fiction, General.

ISBN: 979-8-9908531-3-3 (Paperback)

Printed in the United States of America

To my family who read the first chapter of the first draft and wanted to read more. To my husband who listened to all of my ramblings. And to everyone who took a chance on a little book from a new author. Without you all this book would never have happened.

Life, Death and Everything Else

Contents

Map

SIMKIU
DAETOPOLIS
QUI
SYRENTHIA
BRAETON
TORRICK
HENNIX
NOXID
HAWK'S
FOREST
NORRO
EXELA
SOUTHERN
DESERT

Prequel — Braekios
About 325 Years Ago

It was the cries of the injured that reached me first. I had been traveling, searching for

necromancers, to begin my work with when I came across a quaint town. The small but well-

maintained brick homes had blooming flowers hugging the front door, and the cobblestone road

showed signs of being recently cleaned. It would have been an idyllic place to live, if it weren't

for the mutilated corpses scattered across the ground, blood turning the gray stones a ruddy

brown. A loud scream pierced the air before turning into a low sob. Laughter followed before a

taunting, "Got your nose! Got your nose!" I moved towards where the sound originated, being

sure to step around the bodies, and came across a man in his mid-forties, tawny kinked hair

sticking up at its ends, in mismatching clothing, indeed holding the poor woman's nose. As he

crouched over a young woman and waved the nose tauntingly in her face, his patchwork brown

jacket gaped open and obscured the woman's face, but as he stood back up, I saw terror in her

muddy brown eyes and knew that she was unfortunately human. This was not what I needed, and

I stepped forward to examine the aggressor, hoping that my reason for coming here would not go

unfulfilled.

My foot scuffed against the road as I stepped forward and the subtle sound alerted the

man to my presence. He dropped the oozing nose as he swung to face me, and that is when I saw

its emerald eyes. A smile crept up my face as I pulled out my bow and arrows. I had finally

found a necromancer; my life's work was finally about to begin! I nocked two arrows

simultaneously and aimed for the beast's head. It opened its mouth, no doubt to taunt me, but

with a short *shunk* noise, the arrows found their mark, burying themselves into its eye. The killer collapsed forward, falling onto the unfortunate woman, who tried to crawl backwards without any success, trapping her beneath it. Her shriek continued until I was able to drag her out from underneath the corpse.

The woman muttered a shaking, "Thank you, for saving me," as she tried to stand on shaking legs. I waved her off, leaving her to take care of the deceased around her and began tying up the dead necromancer, readying it and myself for a long, but necessary, journey back home.

The real work began inside my house. Dragging the corpse down into my basement, past the thick wood doors and deeper into the candle lit darkness, I barely contained my excitement. This house, and more importantly my research cells, had taken years for me to build, but I knew it was worth the time and I was eager to put it to use. The walls were thick and would block out any sounds made inside, the floors were made of slick stone, angling towards a small hole in the ground designed to capture loose fluids, such as blood. My doors were thick too, and required several keys to unlock, and stood just out of reach from shackles attached to the walls. All these features were specifically designed with my temporary house guests in mind and now it was time to see how useful they would be. I struggled to lift the now slightly bloated corpse to the table, and I made a note in my journal to find a better way to lift future corpses. My knives and additional tools were laid out, meticulously cleaned, and reflected the torch light off them. I ran a gentle finger down them, thanking them for the service they would provide me. Pressing a knife to the sternum of the necromancer I took a deep breath, my body vibrating with excitement. It was time to begin.

Journal Entry — The necromancer appears human. The body is male and contains all the human genitalia and internal organs. The only noticeable difference is the eyes, which are currently resting in an alcohol/water mixture. I will be examining it daily to see how it reacts to different stimulants.

With nothing left for me to glean from this experiment, I dragged the corpse through the back door to an area cleared of brush and grass. I watched the flames of the fire eat away at the body, and the smell of cooking flesh made me hungry for more work. I allowed myself a week's worth of rest, taking inventory of my supplies and plotting out my next path. I needed to find more necromancers, needed to study them more if I was going to understand their nature. The week came to an end, so I headed out again, traveling west instead of east this time. Thankfully, it only took me two days to come across another necromancer, this one a teenage female. It was relatively easy to knock out and tie up, though it did gain consciousness again halfway through the journey and attempted to run away several times.

The struggle continued until I chained it against the wall of a new cell, bare of the research supplies I had in the first one. I watched through a tiny window near the door for days, seeing how it would react to a lack of water and food, and felt no pity when it begged me for water, its lips cracked and bleeding.

Journal Entry — Despite the Fae blood coursing through the necromancer's system, it needs as much food and water as a human. I had provided the necromancer a single cup of water and when no more was provided it drank its own urine in desperation. It soon perished, in a similar time frame that I would expect a human to perish.

Another journey, another necromancer. My experiment consisted of testing their abilities. I informed the necromancer, an older male, that if they raised the corpse in the room, I would remove a finger. I watched it fight against itself, curling in on itself, pressing hands against the side of its head. Whispered, "don't do it, don't do it, don't do it," leaked from its lips. But all its efforts were for naught. Ten times it raised the dead rabbit in the room, and ten fingers were lost. I made a grave mistake and left the room to make a meal and when I returned, I found that the necromancer had bashed its head against the wall until it lived no more.

I took less risks with the next necromancer, dosing it with a mixture of ground-up moon flowers and water at the end of each research session. The drug kept it unconscious until I was ready to begin with the next experiment. Exploration of their abilities continued, and I introduced more and more corpses in varying stages of decomposition to see how far into the past they could rip a corpse from the clutches of death.

Journal Entry — The necromancer brought back each corpse from animal to human, with exceptions including bug and sea life. As the groupings of corpses grew, it took a larger toll on the necromancer. Red blood dripped out of its eyes and nose when it raised a small group of humans twice the size of the young necromancer.

My knowledge grew and the cells needed daily cleaning. Some may say my soul is damned, but I did what was required to keep us alive. I reached out to those who survived the attacks, sharing my knowledge and inviting them to share my cause, as well as my home. I provided shelter, and food with the promise that they would join me in the battle against necromancy. Slowly, my numbers grew. A division of the strongest fighters was created, their mission to find and bring living necromancers back to the manor. My colleagues and I continued to conduct our experiments, documenting our research for future generations. My most valued members were the children. I molded the youth into my image, teaching them where to strike a necromancer, how to spot the destruction a necromancer wreaks, and more importantly to recognize necromancers not as human but as the monsters they are.

Journal Entry — I write this on my deathbed, one of my students recording it for me. Decades have passed since I began my research and the Order of Braekios has grown. We have observed the necromantic gene being passed down through generations, observing necromancers in the wild as they interact with their own kind. As new offspring came into this world, diluting the Fae blood within it, the necromantic strength they possessed decreased. It is my hope that the necromantic gene will disappear with enough time, but I fear that due to the dominance of the gene that if a drop of Fae blood resides there will always be necromancers.

Chapter One — Lysandra

"There is nothing human about a necromancer. Although they appear humanoid and their blood is red, the destruction that follows them is unique. They serve as a threat, not only to the humans in their way, but to the human species. Therefore, I shall gather all willing and able-bodied to fight for those who cannot."

—Braekios Journal #10, page 13

I walked through the town feeling more at peace than I deserved to be. The weather was warm and sunny, so people walked the streets, smiling as they passed each other and soaked up the sun. I glanced at their faces to see if any had the familiar signs of a population living in fear, tight smiles that didn't reach the eyes, a stiffness in their gait, their paths never straying from the cobblestones that connected the buildings. I anticipated seeing all these signs or at least one, and yet every detail I registered told me that this was a happy, content little town. There was a performer in the main square playing an unfamiliar but upbeat song, dancing close to one audience member before skipping to the next. When he ended, all watching clapped, but none put coins in his waiting hat. I looked closer at the crowd and my eyes caught on dresses with torn hems, kids in pants that fell a little too short on them, and a few gaunt faces belonging to people who could use a good meal or two. I adjusted my assessment of the town to a town that has recently seen hard times but was overall happy. Nothing led me to believe that these people were going to believe why I was here: sent by the Order to investigate, capture and kill the necromancer residing here if the report was accurate.

Let me stop there, for a quick minute. If you're anything like me, you can't stand starting a new story only to be thrust into a scene with little to no context. If you're anything like me, you need a little extra to process new information. If you're anything like me, you want to be able to soak it all in without having to ask questions like, "What's his name? Where are we? What is that? Why is there a smiling three-legged cat rolling down a hill?"

Let me introduce myself. Hi, I'm Lysandra Spits, but most people call me Lys. I was born to people who liked to live large and desperately wanted to be part of the elite. When the influentials in town began to lead "fulfilling lives" with children and couldn't possibly be bothered with those who couldn't understand their struggles, they quickly decided that they simply must have a baby of their own. I came along and after four months they realized that having a kid interfered with their obscenely grandiose parties, which they much more enjoyed, so they dumped me on the doorstep of the only people notorious for taking anyone aged from zero to ninety-nine, the Order of Braekios, or more commonly known as "The Order".

The Order's headquarters was a massive stone building which sat on the largest hill, so my parents easily found it, signed the custody papers, took the twenty coppers they received in exchange for my "service" and left. All before the acolyte could promise that I, "would be well cared for and want for nothing." That evening, Elaine and Hanspeter Spits threw a party like none other, celebrating the child now out of their hands and their re-discovered freedom to focus on whatever their shriveled little hearts wanted. I'd like to say that I was the only child that the Order obtained in this manner, but I was not. Unfortunately, twenty other infants were signed over this way, fortunately this meant that I had twenty new lifelong friends, however long or short that life may be.

If you thought that an organization with a name like the Order would start the indoctrination early, you'd be right! While there isn't much that a four-month-old can do, what it can do is look. The Order provided plenty of colorful pictures for us to absorb, all detailing the evil in the world, mainly in the form of necromancers. Necromancy previously didn't exist in our world, but you know who did? The Fae. Before humans exploded onto the scene, the Fae were there, enjoying having all the land to themselves. Humans appeared, and war broke out, each side wanting to expand their domain and despising the other side. The war was long and the death toll on both sides crept higher each day. Years went by with land being gained and lost, neither side holding onto it long enough to be able to develop it. When it seemed as if the battle would only end when there was no one left to fight it, some hapless human soldier used an iron knife to scratch a Fae across the face. Where a wound like that would normally be shrugged off by the Fae, this time it screamed and clawed at its face. The burn marks and pustules puckered around the scratch was all the soldier needed to see before running off, desperate to tell someone about what happened. The soldier managed to get to his colonel to share his findings, before succumbing to the injuries he acquired. Iron was quickly pulled from wherever it could be found and put into makeshift weapons. Studs from a horse's shoe would be put into a wooden club, turning it from a Fae irritant to a lethal weapon.

Times changed and soon the Fae were extinct. But not before leaving an echo of them that would still be felt centuries later. It seems that while each side claimed to hate the other, some instead fell in love. While these half-breed offspring appeared human (except for the unnatural eyes, usually in every shade except blue, green or brown) they had a unique bastardization of Fae magic, necromancy, and the madness that came with it. Unfortunately for mankind, they didn't inherit their ancestors' opposition to iron and piercing one with something made of iron didn't ensure their death. The next few decades were chaotic, and full of terror. One day you'd be out chatting with your neighbor, and the next your whole town is slaughtered by the skeletal cow remains leftover from the butcher. All because a necromancer wandered into your tiny village by some sort of sick twist of fate. People started to burn anything deceased from livestock and pets to friends and family.

Necromancers ran unstopped until a dude with balls the size of mountains came along. Any guess what his name was? Yup, our good friend Braekios! He did what I will nicely refer to as, "research" them. It was a crap ton of torture that would even have made a Fae turn white. His "research" was well documented, and throughout the centuries the Order existed it was put into multiple mediums, allowing for everyone both inside and outside the Order to read about his journey.

Little Lysandra learned all of this through very graphic picture books shared with her. The books my classmates and I were taught from were so old that I'm sure they'd turn to dust if they ever saw the light of day. As a toddler, most of my time was spent chewing on things I shouldn't, touching things I was told not to, running around naked, and looking at pictures of gruesome murders done by necromancers. My formal education began when I was five, and my days were pretty much the same until I was older. I'd wake up at dawn, along with the seven other girls my age. My class was large thanks to that baby boom, but a lot of acolytes died the previous year from an unusually lethal strain of the wet sickness, so we were able to house the girls in our class in one dorm room and the boys in the other. Once we'd finished making our beds, we'd head to the kitchen. Most of our lives were going to be on the road, so we were expected to be able to provide for ourselves, which meant cooking. At age five, cooking meant making oats and milk but evolved into more elaborate meals as we got cleared to work with the stove and knives. Once dishes were cleared, we'd start the book learning section of the day where classes included history, mathematics, basic medicine, and strategy. Lunch was usually a lighter meal of bread and cold meats eaten in the dining hall before going outside. We'd change into clothes already torn and stained and go into the woods behind us, regardless of if the weather was wet, dry, hot or frigid cold. Once Lucien swore that his pee froze on the tree he peed on because of how cold it was, but I think it was more of an excuse to get out of our exercises instead of the truth.

The trees in the woods were tall and proud, their branches reaching high up towards the sun. The shade they provided had the weeds and occasional shrub fight for the occasional sun ray and rain that would trickle down from the canopy. The hard dirt ground provided a nice flat place for us to practice on, but falling on it always caused loud *oofs* to be forced from our mouths and would send the watching squirrels running for cover. It was in those woods that we developed our skills and put our strategy knowledge to the test. We'd take turns hiding and tracking each other, follow the paths our teachers created, and fight either one-on-one or in groups. When someone broke something, we'd practice setting bones, sewing stitches, and applying poultices. Considering that we never pulled punches and practiced with sharpened weapons, this happened a lot. I still have a scar on my left arm from where Altair very poorly stitched me up after a lost knife fight. When the sun began to set and we all hated each other, it was time to head in for the evening. We'd bathe, eat dinner, and finally have some free time before going to bed and doing it all over the next day. Dinah, Niamh and I would usually climb up onto the roof to look at the stars, sometimes talking about whichever classmate drove us crazy that day, but usually we'd sit in silence, huddling together against the breeze, happy to just be in the same space since graduation grew closer with every passing second.

Twenty-three was a significant number for the Order. The war fought between the Fae and the humans lasted for twenty-three years before coming to a bloody end. The rest of the nation considered a child an adult when they turned eighteen, but for the Order it was when we turned twenty-three. All our classes and experiences came together in one final brutal test. We were given one weapon, which we picked out only after inspecting it with a scrutinizing view, as well as one change of clothes, one flint, and one week to track and kill a necromancer. It was only when we returned with the unnatural eyes that we became graduates of the Order, known as chasseurs. I was lucky, my tracking skills lead me to an old necromancer traveling by itself.

From the back, the hunched over form with gray hair and a walking stick could be mistaken for an elderly woman, but as soon as she turned around at my, "Excuse me miss, could you help me?" The yellow eyes gave it away for what it was. There wasn't much of a fight, I'm almost ashamed to say, and I managed to kill it and remove its eyes (a nasty practice if you ask me) without getting so much as a scratch. Not all my classmates were as lucky as me though, some had missing digits or spent weeks in the infirmary, while the ones who couldn't kill a necromancer were forced to try the test again the following month.

There was no leaving the Order once you joined, the ones who failed the first time repeated the test until they either succeeded or died. Our names were stamped into the weapon we used to kill the necromancer with reminders of what we did and proof that the Order didn't waste its resources on us. As a reward we were given our own apartments in the buildings adjacent to the main Order manor to reside in when not out hunting down necromancers. My hatchet has my name stamped into the handle, though I grew fond of brass knuckles after the ritual and tended to use them more frequently than my hatchet. These weapons weren't used during training and were kept safe by the weapons master until we went on a hunt. If we survived or died during a clash against a necromancer would come down to our strength and how good our weapons were, so we were required to inspect them at least twice a week to ensure that they were sharp and clean.

Chapter Two — Lysandra

"Anything that once breathed can serve as a weapon for a necromancer. A bird or a wolf can kill as easily as a human under a necromancer's control. Time is the only thing that makes the difference. The longer something has remained dead, the harder it is for a necromancer to reanimate it."

—Braekios Journal #1, page 143

Mere weeks after graduation we were once again put to the test. Niamh, Dinah and I were exercising outside, alternating between hand-to-hand combat and weapon drills, surrounded by a few other chasseurs doing similar activities, when our old weapons teacher Ms. Hannah came running. Lips pressed tightly together; hands clenched down by her side told us that something important was coming our way. We gathered around her as she sighed and said grimly, "We are all being summoned into the hall. Once we arrive, the Preceptor will address you."

As we walked back, Dinah and Niamh drifted over to me, both sets of eyes wide and I could feel the tension bounce between us. In silence, we reentered the building and immediately stopped upon reaching the hall. I looked around seeing infants in the arms of their teachers and a few of the older acolytes who were on the verge of graduating. Apparently, it wasn't just us being summoned, but all the chasseurs and acolytes currently in residence. I heard the tell-tale "ahem" as Preceptor Maren, the headmaster of this branch, stepped up to the dais in front of the hall.

Now, although I call him Preceptor Maren, I am fully convinced that this man is Braekios himself, despite Braekios being buried in the woods behind the manor. If someone had told me that this man fought in the great battle all those centuries ago, I would have easily believed them, the Preceptor is that old. With every step that Preceptor Maren takes, his body trembles as if the only thing propelling him forward is his sheer will to move and live. The Preceptor has been completely hairless for as long as I can remember, even eyelashes were missing from him, as if his body is a loose sack of wrinkles that nothing could stick to. Lucien and I used to guess how many times Preceptor Maren would blink during the length of a conversation and then we'd go talk to him to see who was the closest. We always seemed to guess too low. The only thing older than Preceptor Maren is the Order's building I called home. While the Order has branches all over the continent, this was the one Braekios built himself and where the first acolytes of the Order studied. There are still rooms in the basement that have finger-sized gouged marks in the doors and floors tinted red. We grew up knowing that the walls used to be pretty river stones in different shades of blue, brown and gray, but it was difficult to believe since now they were all in the same shade of old people gray. The Order never had excess money, relying on donations and charity and this meant that the meager money it did have went to ensuring that its chasseurs had enough to live off. When leaks inevitably sprung during the rainy season it was our job to patch them up instead of replacing the roof, and our beds had deep dents in them from their previous owners.

"Ahem," said Preceptor Maren, and the force of this caused a coughing attack that had all of us gathered wondering if this was truly the time that he would die.

When the coughs subsided, he spoke, his blinking accentuating every syllable. "I wish that I could share good news, but we have received news that Qui now has a living population of zero."

We all inhaled sharply at this news. Qui was a mid-sized town about two and a half days northwest and was a major exporter of the wool that most of the common people made into clothing as well as blankets and other linens.

"A man went to visit his daughter and her new husband and found all the townspeople dead. He immediately sent us a raven," the Preceptor continued, his grave look offset by the slight trembling caused by the turning of his head. "As we are the closest branch, it falls on us to respond. However, I recognize that sending just one person to track such a lethal necromancer is to court death, so we will be forming a team of six. As this is most time sensitive, if you are chosen, expect to leave tonight. For now, you are dismissed. The teachers and I will be discussing who to send and they will inform you of our selections." With that the Preceptor left, along with the teachers of the older classes trailing behind him, already deep in discussion.

With nothing to do for the rest of the day, most of us drifted back to our apartments to play cards or to share speculations regarding the mission. I found myself in a game of cards with Dinah, Niamh, Lucien and Altair, all of us paying more attention to the footsteps in the hallway than the game we were playing.

"I bet Stephen will be the medic. I never hear the teachers say anything negative about him." We all nodded our agreement to Altair's whispered words; Stephen co-taught our medicine classes despite being our senior by only two years.

"I wonder who else is going. I'm not sure that I would want to be a part of the team, even if it meant a chance to leave Braeton," Niamh said after slapping the pile one last time to win the game.

We all groaned and stood up to stretch muscles stiff from sitting hunched over. As we sat back down to play a different game our combat teacher, Ms. Sydra, came in, eyes sweeping over us gathered in the room. I felt her eyes settle on me and prepared to stand up. "Lysandra, Dinah, come speak with me," she said, already striding back into the hallway.

There was only one reason we'd be pulled aside, and as we stood to leave the room Niamh gripped our hands and kissed them gently. "Please, please be safe and come back to me. Both of you."

I gave her a smile way more confident than I felt and Dinah nodded in typical quiet Dinah-fashion.

"Don't worry Niamh, Dinah will keep me safe." Dinah rolled her eyes, used to playing the role of mother within our trio, and we followed Ms. Sydra down to the other apartment wing.

Just as we caught up to her, she stopped in front of Xavier's door.

"Why did it have to be Xavier?" Dinah whispered to me, disgust lacing her words.

I had to agree with her. Xavier was the human equivalent of sweaty armpits, he always lingered way too long, seemed to always smell a little off, and wasn't really liked by anyone. His greasy brown hair and pimply face didn't do anything to add to his likeability and his sneer of a smile always had me wondering if punching him in the face would make him more attractive. The only thing this walking cloud of body odor had going for him was that he was the best medic in our graduating class. Unfortunately for my nostrils, this guy could reattach a butterfly's wing in the back of a bumpy wagon.

We gave him a slight wave as he joined us and received a smirk in return. We re-entered the main hall to find another small group assembled composed of Stephen, and two others— Anowen and Dorian. I was surprised to see Anowen and Dorian, they both graduated early and were usually out on missions, it was unusual that they were in residence.

We turned to our teacher at her sigh, and she rubbed her forehead saying, "I'm sure you all have figured it out by now, but you are the group that will be hunting down the necromancer. You all know your skills and where you fit in, I'm not going to tell you what to do. I do suggest that you figure out who is going to be making the executive decisions in case you disagree on what path you'll take. This mission will not allow for anything except the killing of the necromancer responsible for the desecration of Qui. Go, gather your belongings, and meet back here in an hour. Don't forget to stop by the weapons master and select your weapons."

As we all returned to our apartments to pack, classmates gathered around Dinah and me, eager to learn about the mission and who else would be going. We were assaulted by questions, but one look from Dinah had everyone except Niamh finding something more interesting to do. With our backpacks heavy with the gear we needed, Dinah and I exchanged one last goodbye with Niamh.

"Make sure you kill this monster, Lys. And stay out of trouble, okay? I don't need you to come back wounded because you pissed off one of the others," Niamh said gently as we embraced, our foreheads touching lightly.

"I promise, we'll come back. In one piece. Try not to worry too much," I said in return as I pulled back, shouldering my backpack.

I felt the tears gather but looked away, determined to not let Niamh see my anxiety. I heard Niamh let out a slight sob as she embraced Dinah. I didn't catch what was said between the two of them, but when I turned back, I saw tears in both of their eyes.

"Let's go," I said to Dinah, my voice rougher than it should have been.

We went down to the armory, run by a tiny, stout woman who took care of our weapons and kept everything organized, and I watched as Dinah gathered her weapon of choice, daggers.

Dinah may not look like a fighter, but her tall, lithe form ensured that she was faster than anyone who got in her way. I've seen her make an opponent bleed from three different areas by the time that person realized they needed to turn around. I could never beat her when it came to speed, but where she was fast, I was strong. I used my strength and endurance to wear down my opponent and used weapons best suited for close combat.

While we practiced with a multitude of weapons and were expected to carry at least one ranged weapon and one for close combat, I have always gravitated towards brass knuckles. There was something so satisfying about feeling a bone crunch beneath your knuckles. I couldn't stand to watch the dancing some people do during a fight; I much preferred planting my feet and having a brawl until one of us falls unconscious. I collected my knuckles, my engraved hatchet, which I could either throw or wield in my off hand, and a few knives for preparing dinner (or cutting Xavier if he got too close to me) and followed Dinah out into the hall.

All six of us were gathered in the hall but we shifted on our feet awkwardly in the thick silence that grew around us, waiting for someone to take the lead. That sure as hell wasn't going to be me, I'm not the best planner, and I liked to trust my instinct instead of listening to my brain. It wasn't a problem when I was by myself, I knew how to extradite myself from a sticky situation, but I didn't want to be the reason this group didn't return.

I was on the verge of breaking the silence with an ill-timed joke as Anowen finally spoke. "Here's how this is going to go. We'll travel to Qui and start tracking the necromancer from there. Dorian, Dinah, as the strategists, we'll expect you to come up with the battle formation for when we do intercept it. Stephen, you and Xavier will need to take stock of our inventory and make sure none of our medicine and poultices go bad on the journey. You won't really be needed until after we encounter the necromancer, obviously, but I still expect you to pull your weight until then. Call it what you'd like, but my intuition is telling me that we'll acquire quite a few wounds as we go, and we'll need you two to be able to help. Lys and I will oversee setting the pace we travel at until we get to Qui. Once there, we'll work to find the path of the necromancer and lead us to them. I know we're all eager to prove ourselves, especially since this is the younger ones' first mission since graduation, but let's remember that we can't do that if we're dead." She let out a long breath. "Let's go."

"Well, that was some kind of speech," I murmured to Dinah as we left the Order. "I'm not sure I'd call it motivational."

I got a slight chuckle from Dinah who responded with, "I'm pretty sure she practiced it every day since she joined the Order. On the off chance that she'd get a chance to make a speech." She may have said it in a low voice, but it was a wasted effort because I let out a massive snort that had everyone turning their heads to stare at us, questioning.

After several rolled eyes we walked with the intention of stopping when the sun started to set. We all stayed true to Anowen's plan, with us stopping once Anowen declared we made enough progress. That night, Dinah and Dorian caught some rabbits, and we had one last hot meal, knowing that we wouldn't be lighting any more fires to prevent the necromancer from being alerted to our presence. The next day was full of laughter and jokes about our teachers and the Preceptor. With the sun shining, birds singing a merry tune and the crunch of twigs and acorns beneath our shoes, it was easy to forget why we were all together.

I've always enjoyed being outside and away from the lifeless stones of the Order. In the woods, I could look at a broken branch or some tiny footprints and know exactly what came by and the life it led, but people were harder to figure out. Animals also never left a dead fish under my bed as a prank. As we settled down for the night, our good moods disappeared with the sinking sun. Qui would be reached mid-day tomorrow and then the real work would begin. After dinner, we all split up to double check our weapons and armor. Once done, we laid down on our mats and tried to fall asleep. Sleep eluded me though, and I rolled from side to side trying to quiet my racing mind and restless legs. After someone gave a not-so-subtle *harump*, I got up and walked away from camp. I ran fighting drills over and over until my arms were too heavy to lift and my mind stopped thinking about the what ifs. I returned to camp drenched in sweat and collapsed into a dreamless sleep.

The next morning, we silently packed up, not a word shared between us, and nothing needing to be said. We left camp and I looked for signs of the necromancer's path, though not anticipating seeing anything. I did it more out of habit, my training drilled into me. When it became apparent I had an aptitude for tracking and the memory for it as well, I was sent out alone in the woods to track a path created by a teacher. They'd walk into the woods, being sure to leave the occasional footprint, rustling leaves as they passed, and breaking branches. At the end of their walk a cloth would be tied, to mark the end of my radius. I'd follow the path and then report back once I returned, forced to retell every animal scat I passed, every type of fallen tree that was around me, the directions I took… Anything and everything that might be informational. If I failed to remember something, or if it was deemed too little detail, I was sent back into the woods. The older I got, the longer and more subtle the paths became. One particularly long path created for me took a month of going back out before my teacher decided I remembered enough. Now, I stored information instinctively, those skills coming as easy to me as breathing.

Anowen's sudden stop pulled me out of my head and almost into her back. We gathered around her as she pointed to a pile of stones saying, "Qui is just an hour away. I'd prefer for us to be warmed up and rested before entering the city, so we'll take a quick break here. Do you what you need to do to prepare."

We began our own rituals. Preparation in the Order meant being both physically and mentally prepared. A fight could be determined by whoever lost focus first, so we trained to make sure our attention never strayed. This was accomplished by slipping into what we called, "the killer's calm" and it looked different for everyone. Dinah, for example, would focus on the movement of her daggers as they rolled over her knuckles, and she'd slowly pick up speed. I could almost go into a trance myself watching her fingers, so I understood why she did it. My preferred method was to take a moment to close my eyes and imagine myself at a lake I came across one time when I was camping during a week of free time. In my mind, I'm walking through the woods, following a winding dirt path to a lake with crystal blue waters and the sun reflecting off the surface. The water in the lake is so still that even a slight breeze from the wind causes a ripple to travel across it. Only when I feel my mind calm and focused do I open my eyes and prepare my body, taking care to stretch not just my arms, but my legs and back as well. My soft wool travel clothes are switched out for stiffer leather ones that have reinforced spots on the chest, and a tall hard leather collar that reaches around my neck and up to the bottom of my ears. I readied my hands, popping my knuckles (a bad habit, but one I can't seem to break) and by the time I was limber and aching to move forward, the rest of the group was finishing up their stretches. The last thing we did was strap on our weapons, my brass knuckles clicking into place on gloves designed to prevent them from slipping off. Those gloves were the only thing I owned that could be seen as valuable. The Order owned us and our gear until we earned enough to buy our own, but Niamh and Dinah had pooled money earned from taking odd jobs in the town to gift me these for my birthday. My hatchet I strapped onto my left hip to be wielded by my dominant hand.

Properly geared up, we walked again, taking care to make no noise that would give us away. While we didn't anticipate the necromancer still being in Qui, we didn't want to alert anyone or anything to our presence, regardless of if they would be friend or foe. There was a feeling of absolute wrongness that let us know we made it to Qui. There were no bird or animal noises, no wind, no movement. There was nothing except the feeling and the smell. The nauseating, sickly sweet smell of rotting bodies seemed to seep into our bodies and override our senses. As for the taste the smell created in my mouth, well, let's just say that I haven't eaten meat since that day. Xavier went pale, vomiting into a nearby bush, and I heard Dorian gagging quietly. I felt the bile rising in my throat, but I was determined not to join them. I sank back into my mind, running instead of walking to that lake and slowly overcame the urge to be sick.

Anowen saw the state that we were in, half of us still bent over heaving, and gave out orders to try to regroup, saying, "Stephen, Xavier, look for survivors. I doubt we'll find any, but we want to do our due diligence. Dinah, Dorian, I'm sorry for the task I'm going to give you… Please gather any of the bodies you can find into one pile near the center of the city. Lys and I will examine the scene and figure out where the abomination who did this went."

We tied clothes over our noses and mouths, hoping to keep the smell and taste of death at bay, and went to work. I joined Anowen who studied the nearby body of a young boy around twenty who stared up at the sky with his neck opened in a gory smile and endless pits where the eyes should be.

"Did he fight against the necromancer?" I muttered, bending down next to her.

She didn't look at me when she responded. "No, there are no defensive wounds. Look at these wounds." She gestured to a tight grouping of small, deep holes. "They're too sharp to have been done by fingers. Not to mention that it looks like the eyes were the first thing to go." The eye sockets were further along in the stages of decay than the rest of the body, and despite the gouge marks there was no evidence that other animals had been eating this corpse.

"Birds?" I asked, looking around but not seeing any beyond the loose feathers scattered across the ground.

She nodded. "The birds attacked so that he'd be distracted while the necromancer killed him. Look at the angle of the slash mark on his neck. Someone shorter than him attacked from the front. The only way he wouldn't have fought back is if he couldn't have seen his attacker."

Now I know what you're thinking, out of all living and dead things, why birds? People burn corpses of livestock, people, and pets. But what is a relatively common prey animal that can be found among wild and populated areas that is easily killed? Birds. Predators aren't courteous enough to eat the entirety of a bird, so a necromancer wouldn't have to look very hard to find enough remains to reanimate it. Birds are also inconspicuous enough that most wouldn't notice them until one attacked their face. What is surprising is the amount of damage done by a swarm of them. Qui wasn't tiny, around two hundred people lived here during the warmer seasons, fall winter had most taking their flocks further down south. The only way this was possible was if the necromancer caught the town unaware and reanimated the people it killed immediately and forced dead relatives to turn on the living, slowly adding to the army. It was difficult to tell how many corpses it may have used in the attack since the bodies were spread throughout Qui, but it did mean that the necromancer likely would still be accompanied by a few corpses.

With the mystery of how it happened pretty much solved, it was time to find the path. We started by walking in circular paths, moving opposite of each other, walking down different pathways as we encountered them, while looking for signs that the necromancer had passed there. Blood, feathers, drag marks, anything. The first sign I encountered was a door thrown open to a small well-built house, where flowers still bloomed in windowsill boxes. I entered the house and didn't see anyone, living or dead.

Maybe they got away, I thought as I opened the door to the backyard.

I almost laughed when I came across the remains of a mother and her daughter who looked as if they slumbered if not for the chain of gouge marks on their throats. Of course, they didn't get away. No one ever gets away from a necromancer, regardless of how weak that necromancer is or the type of corpse it uses. I steeled myself to do what I knew had to come next. Grabbing the wrist of the mother and child, I dragged them through the house, the street, and to the mass grave Dorian and Dinah had started.

The sight of bodies stacked five high with more arriving drove me to my knees. It was one thing to hear that the town was slaughtered, but it was another to see it. Rage coursed through my body turning my blood molten. How dare they. How dare anyone or anything cut a life short. No matter how large or small a person lived, life was full of vibrancy and color, all coming together to form a story passed down through generations. This necromancer erased them all. We would never know who these women, men, and children would become or the knowledge they had learned. There was so much potential needlessly thrown away. Countless lovers and family members miles away would always question what had happened. Sure, the gossip would spread, but people were hopeful, and until they were confronted with the truth, their hearts would ache with the optimism that their person was still alive. I was determined to take the life of the creature that did this. These monsters weren't human, were barely even things, and would get treated with the same courtesy they treated these lives.

I continued to stare at the grave, the image burning into my soul, and I slowly noticed a path of fresh footprints leading down the only path I hadn't walked yet. A small set led the way for a set of six dragging footprints. I dragged myself up and went to follow the feet, seeing where they led. Every few yards I came across the same footprints and found some feathers resting on a tree branch. I walked until I couldn't see the city, following a trail of broken sticks, leaves, and the occasional loose bird feather, before I was certain I was on the right path. I marked the path I traveled with sticks as I returned to the city, smoke making the smell of death even more repugnant. By the time I returned, night had fallen and the fire in the center was the only thing casting light on the rest of the group. Anger was a shared sentiment amongst the rest of them and we were all eager to leave this place.

Anowen looked up from the fire as I approached her.

"I found the path," I said quietly.

"You're certain? I don't want us to waste time we don't have."

I nodded and straightened as she turned to the rest of the group.

"Lys has the necromancer's scent. I know we're all tired, but I also know that we're all eager to punish the beast that did this. Let's channel that anger and use it. The monster lived its last day, and we can rest once it's dead."

I watched as their faces sharpened with resolve as Dorian spoke. "We've trained for this. We don't know how many corpses the necromancer may have revived, but the necromancer remains the larger threat. Dinah and I will engage with the necromancer directly. Anowen, hang back and use your bow to pick off any stragglers getting in our way. Lys, you're going to keep Stephen and Xavier safe. We'll need their skills once this is all over. I know that this thing has had a head start, but they need sleep like the rest of us. If we move quickly and are incredibly lucky, we might catch it unaware. Take a moment to center yourselves. This is going to be a long, rough night, but we have a duty to those who died."

We left to gather our wits once more and prepared ourselves for a long night. Xavier was the last one to regroup with us, looking way paler and more shaken than any of us. I led us out of Qui, following the path I had memorized but still marked. We walked in a brisk march that soon had us all sweating, but time was not on our side. The trail was winding, and it appeared as if the necromancer had no destination, until we found ourselves at a fork in the road and a familiar sign. Daetopolis still a few days walk to the northeast but Braeton a day away. We needed to stop the necromancer before it brought chaos and destruction to our home. A quick glance around us showed me a broken twig just off the road confirming the direction they traveled in and confirmed our fear; the necromancer was heading to Braeton.

We quickly followed the path and found ourselves deep in the woods when I came to a stop, causing Dorian to step on my heel. I lifted a closed fist into the air, our sign for absolute silence. I directed Dorian's eyes to what I had noticed, a pair of shoes, barely peeking through the bushes. Dorian held up an open fist, the sign for battle formation and we fell into position, waiting for him to give the signal to engage. We hadn't seen any additional bodies on our walk here, and it was weird that we didn't see any in the clearing, but I shrugged it off. We anticipated fighting whatever corpses the necromancer had, so not knowing the exact number in the clearing didn't put fear into my heart. Maybe the necromancer gave the order for them to wander away, which would mean they'd be causing chaos elsewhere. Still a problem, but once we killed the necromancer, the corpses would collapse wherever they were.

When his hand dropped, we inched in and circled the sleeping necromancer, looking around for corpses, but not seeing any. As we prepared to strike, two things happened at once. Six corpses burst from the loose dirt we had walked past, and we were all restrained from behind, the corpses pinning our arms to our sides. My fingertips brushed my hatchet, but I couldn't pull it out of its sheath or break free from the grasp that held me. The necromancer, a damned child, rose from where it was sleeping and looked over us. Its clothing was slightly torn but was clearly expensive, visible in the deep navy hue of its pants and in the rich emerald shirt that collected with little frills at the wrists and throat. Its fine brown hair was pulled back into a ponytail keeping it away from the slightly angular face, but time had taken a toll on it and strands escaped the leather strap holding it. If I came across this thing on the street, I'd assume it was a young lordling who never strayed from his oversized city home. It wasn't until the light from the small fire reflected off its eyes that I saw the madness. There wasn't a drop of humanity in those orange eyes, nothing except the eerie light that the Fae used to have, turning them into amber.

It angled its head and counted us. "One, two, three, four, five, six! Oh, I know! Let's play a game! Eenie meenie miney mo." The eyes narrowed. "You two got to go!"

Without so much as a gesture, the necks of Dinah and Stephen were snapped, and their bodies fell to the ground with soft plops. I heard nothing, not the horrified cries from the rest of the group or the ecstatic chuckle of the creature as it skipped around us, stopping to peer up into our faces, only an endless ringing.

Do something, I screamed at my frozen body. I trained, didn't I? All those years in the woods, all those cuts and broken bones meant I learned something, right? I tried to command my legs to move or for my fingers to dig into my captor's arms, but nothing responded. I finally looked at the rest of the group and held Anowen's eyes through the flames. Her eyes were wide with terror, but as she took a deep breath, her eyes calmed, and I knew the only thing she saw was the threat in front of her. I followed her lead, taking some deep breaths to calm my racing heart and shaky breathing. I acknowledged all the useless thoughts floating through my head and let them move past me like ripples across my lake. Soon, my head was empty except for the sound of the dying fire crackling, and the way the rough texture of the corpse's shirt felt against the back of my neck.

With my last exhale, I bent my head down, as if in submission to my fate, and quickly brought it back up, slamming it into the face of the corpse holding me. It stumbled but didn't drop me and I was dragged backwards. Dirt gathered at my heels, and I scrambled for purchase. I did the only thing I could think of, grabbing hold of the arms circling me before quickly sinking to the ground, falling into a crouching position ready to fight. The corpse didn't anticipate a change in my lateral position, and as it looked down at me with a cocked angle to its large bald head, I finally got a look at what had been restraining me. The straight line across the throat of the mid-aged man who held me supported our theory that the necromancer surprised Qui's citizens, instead of overpowering them. The corpse was still in his nightwear, no doubt he was killed while sleeping and reanimated before he could change clothes. It was almost comical the way it looked down at me between its arms, still hugging air, and I swore I saw confusion in its dead gaze. Rising to my feet, my fist contacted the face still angled down towards me. With a glorious *crack,* the chin broke, the head forced to face the sky, and I wasted no time in attacking again.

If you think I showed any mercy to this thing that was once human, you'd be sorely wrong. I channeled my fear, anger, and sorrow into making sure that my brass knuckles connected with the corpse's head. Repeatedly. Judging by the sounds around me, mayhem had taken our well-intended plan and made it unachievable. I didn't let my eyes linger on Dinah and Stephen as I looked for the others. Xavier was nowhere that I could see, probably hiding somewhere and acting dead, the fucking coward. Yet the corpse of a gangly teenage boy, who originally held him, was on the ground and missing everything below the knees. Maybe I should give Xavier more credit than I normally do, but now was not the time to start considering that.

Anowen held her own against a large, deceased man twice her size, dodging attacks from the massive branch this dead beast managed to rip off a tree, but Dorian faced off against two corpses and was on the defensive. He twisted away from one blow from the tall woman with matted blonde hair, only to be sent stumbling forward from a kick sent to his back by an equally tall man who must have been the woman's sibling. Watching him fight would have been a great opportunity to learn more about sword fighting if I hadn't found myself dodging sporadic slashes from the necromancer, who had pulled two knives from Stephen's pockets. Out of the corner of my eye, I saw Dorian kill the larger corpse that had been the one to land a kick on him with a swift decapitation. Yet, in the next second Dorian's body fell to the ground, and his head was in the hands of the other corpse who faced him. There was a look of permanent surprise on Dorian's decapitated head and blood dripped down it, onto his cooling body. I tried not to consider how little of a chance we stood at survival if our two best fighters were dead.

The necromancer ran over to examine the body, kicking at it gently. "There goes another one," it laughed, making eye contact with me. "You guys are pretty weak, aren't ya?" I rolled my eyes but refused to converse with it.

Anowen's victorious cry marked the removal of another corpse from the fight. There was a shriek from behind a nearby bush and I recognized it as Xavier's, having heard it plenty of times growing up, usually right as he was pinned down by an opponent. Anowen stalked towards the source of the shriek, no doubt to help Xavier against whatever foe he faced. I followed Anowen, when the small terror of a necromancer leaped on her back and stabbed at any exposed skin, drawing blood with every successful swipe. The sudden weight and onslaught had Anowen stumbling, and I sped up to assist. I caught up and wrapped my arms around its small frame, pulling it off Anowen. Backing up with the necromancer in my arms it turned to hiss at me before I threw it as far away from me as I could manage. Landing on its feet gracefully, no doubt thanks to the unnatural finesse its ancestors once had, it held a chunk of Anowen's face in its hand that dripped blood, raising the piece to its mouth to lick it.

Anowen didn't turn to look at me as she stumbled forward towards the loud moans coming from Xavier, a corpse trailing behind her slowly.

"Anowen, behind you!" I shouted as the necromancer stared at me, a gleeful look in its eyes.

She turned and her daggers streaked through the air before dislocating the shoulders attached to the hands that grabbed at her. Successfully managing to live for another couple of seconds, she disappeared into the tall grass that hid Xavier.

The necromancer advanced, slashing motions controlled but picking up speed as it skipped towards me, the knives reached out in front of itself. I waited until it was within my reach before attempting to land a jab across its face. Before I made contact, a bird popped into my vision and moved to peck at my eyes, causing me to reflect the blow to the bird instead of the necromancer. With every swing of my hatchet or attempted punch, a bird was there to reposition me. I was forced to dodge not just the necromancer's daggers but the nuisance birds too. It was all I could do to avoid getting hit.

There was another loud scream from the grass, and as the necromancer turned to look, I saw my opportunity. My vision narrowed to that moment, the necromancer occupying sole residency in my mind. I ran forward and used my hatchet to knock the dagger out of its right hand. I prepared a right hook that would have put an end to the fight when I felt a searing pain on the side of my face that had me stumbling back. I reached my hand up and found a gaping hole where my left ear normally was. As the blood dripped down my face and made the ground slick my vision widened painfully, and I saw the last reanimated corpse swaying next to me. I felt rather than saw the necromancer and the corpse who seemed smug despite being dead approach me, and I swung out blindly, barely hitting the necromancer. I made enough contact to send it tripping over a rock and falling to the floor. The corpse was less fortunate and despite my vision growing blurrier by the second, I made direct contact with it. As it doubled over, I used my hatchet to quickly remove its limbs and then its head. It was only then that I realized the corpse I had re-killed was the one hunting after Anowen.

If I had killed the corpse, where was Anowen? I didn't have to look too hard before spotting a trail of blood slowly seeping out from the bushes. I didn't need to see her body to know that she was dead, the amount of blood that I saw was too valuable for her to live without. The previous rage took over me and my vision narrowed to the cause of so much unnecessary suffering. The necromancer must have seen my eyes burn with a dark fire, because it pouted, trying to use its young age to make me feel pity. Instead, it fed my righteous fury and I advanced. It opened its mouth to speak to me as I got closer, but with a single strong front kick, it fell to the ground. Incapable of speaking without air in its lungs it could only gape at me. Nothing stopped my advance, not the blood dripping from the new hole in my head, the way my vision began to grow darker by the second, nor the remaining reanimated birds taking their pound of flesh from my face.

I saw its round eyes dart around, looking for anything to use to defend itself, but I had picked up Dinah's daggers as I approached. Large, pitiful eyes leaked tears above a wobbling lip, but I recognized it for what it was—one last attempt at forcing me to see it as human instead of the monster it was. I refused to buy into its act and twirled the daggers in my hands, enjoying the slow advance of fear across the necromancer's face. Pulling out Dinah's daggers felt like closure. This thing killed Dinah; it was only fair that it was killed by her weapons. "Mercy," it tried to say, but I plunged the daggers through its hands and deep into the ground and a scream was the only thing it could get out. I let the necromancer squirm beneath me for a bit. Let it try to escape only to tear bigger holes in its hands before stopping, reduced to tears. I felt a smile come to my face and knew that it was all teeth. I felt good. I felt powerful and just. This creature had caused pain to those I held dear and those who had their own to hold dear, it was only fair that it felt the agony it caused in its last minutes.

I savored the way its body trembled, the way its face grew white from blood loss and the way it stared up at me in horror. I saw the lights in its eyes begin to fade and it was only then that I granted it any kind of mercy. I raised my foot, still encased in its metal toe boot we all wore as part of our gear and brought it down on my prey's face. Like a spoon hitting wet oats, the head splattered against the ground. I heard soft plops as the remaining dead birds fell to the ground, no longer attached to a life-force through magic.

I fell to the ground then, the wounds and blood loss finally catching up to me as I called out to Xavier. "It's over, come out."

"I—I can't see the way out," was the whispered, stuttered reply.

Rolling my eyes, I pulled myself back to my feet. "Fine, swing your knives around and I'll find you."

I heard and saw the tall grass swish in response and started my way towards him, finally walking past the body of Anowen, a look of surprise still on her face. The moon was full and illuminating the whole clearing; Xavier was making an excuse instead of facing the result of his cowardness.

"Your guide and savior is—" I said sarcastically before choking on my words.

Xavier would carry marks from this fight with him all his life, as would I. If I didn't know that Xavier had been with us, I wouldn't have been able to identify the person I saw in front of me as him. Chunks of flesh were missing from his face and hands, and it was clear that he took most of the bird's attacks instead of the rest of the team. What wasn't a gaping hole was completely swollen, distorting his face almost to the point that it was as round and pocketed as the moon in the sky. The bridge of his nose was all that remained of his sneering face, the cartilage completely gone. Yet none of that was the worst. Where his brown eyes had once been were now empty pits, the insides so red it was as if all that remained of his soul was slowly oozing out.

"Is it bad?" He asked, slumped down in front of me.

He reached his hands up to touch his face, but I grabbed them and squeezed gently, hoping to still his trembling and mine. I took a shaky breath before responding, "It's not too bad. It looks like something got you in the eyes, which is probably why your vision is poor, but it's nothing they can't fix at the Order." I couldn't tell if he believed me or not. "I'm a little beat up too, let's bandage our wounds and head out tomorrow with the daylight. Where are your supplies?"

Xavier pointed a shaking finger towards his pack a few feet away from us and I found his supplies, bandaging us up, and hoped that the herbs I used would prevent the inevitable infections. I led us to a spot under some trees, well away from the scent of the corpses now rotting again. Xavier, with his hands on my shoulders, followed right behind me, and his unsteady breath in my remaining ear was the only noise he made outside of the occasional whimper. I propped Xavier against a tree and gave him food and water, and finally took inventory of my body. Besides my now missing ear, which had decided to give me a nonstop splitting headache and dizziness, I was unscathed. Sure, I'd have some cuts that would scar, and it would be a miracle if I could move tomorrow without groaning, but I'd live. I'd live. I. Would. Live. The thought rattled around in my brain, making a hollow noise and I realized I was one of the only ones who walked away from that encounter. Did the Preceptor know he sent us out to die? I let out a tiny sob as my shock finally wore off and I realized that I would never see Dinah again. A louder sob that couldn't be stifled escaped my lips and Xavier picked up his head from where I assumed he was sleeping.

"What happened?" His voice was dull and flat, completely devoid of any emotion.

"The necromancer prepared a trap. It had corpses with it, besides birds, because we are fucking stupid and forgot to count the bodies at Qui. Six corpses grabbed us before we were able to attack."

Xavier nodded, showing he remembered.

"I don't remember what happened next." I lied, this night would be a source of nightmares for years to come, but at that moment I couldn't voice any of it. "All I know is that by the time the necromancer was killed, you and I were the only ones left." It was silent after that, and I thought he had gone back to sleep.

"My eyes aren't going to heal, are they?" Xavier asked hopelessly, and I gulped.

"Of course they are! It's not too bad!" I tried to lace my words with the optimism I didn't feel, but the words rang false in my ears.

"Don't fucking lie to me!" He screamed, his hands now going to his face, fingers finding those holes and pressing into them, fresh blood pooling around his fingertips. "You can't heal what isn't there! Trust me, I would know." His hands dropped and his head fell back against the tree. "What am I going to do now? I can't be a medic if I can't see, I can't even go to the bathroom if I can't find my way." His hands fell to where his knives resided at his side and his fingertips gently caressed the sharp points of the blades. He shuddered slightly when it pricked his skin, and I watched a drop of blood well up.

"What are you doing?" I whispered as he slowly raised it to his throat.

"Tell them that five of us died tonight," was all he said before he jerked the dagger harshly across his throat. Screaming, I stumbled to my feet and lunged towards him, but I was only able to catch his falling, quickly cooling body. His head slumped forward, and the blood poured from the wound in thick wet drops.

I never liked Xavier, but someone did. He had friends, I had overheard that he even had a girlfriend in town, and now they'd have a gap in their lives no one would be able to fill.

I didn't wait until the next morning to bring Xavier back to the others and put them all to rest. I laid them on top of each other gently, after removing their weapons, and prepared the pyre. I don't believe in a god, couldn't believe that some omnipotent being would allow for such pain to exist, but I do believe in holding onto a piece of theirs to look upon when you want to hold onto their memory.

Once I had gathered all the weapons (Dinah's small dagger, Dorian's short sword, Anowen's bow, Stephen's axe, and Xavier's knife), I lit the fire and watched as the flames first at the clothing and then the bodies of my friends.

"You were all important, to the Order and to me. You traded your life for the scores of others who now get to see another sunrise. I will talk of your bravery, and your sacrifice. I've learned so much from you and I'll think of you with every jab of my fists and every swing of my hatchet." There was nothing more I could say, and I had to swallow the lump that formed in my throat. "Goodbye, everyone. I'll miss you."

I turned away and began my slow, limping journey back to the Order, the weapons in my bag weighing me down almost as much as the knowledge that I'd have to report on what happened here. By the time the twinkling lights of Braeton were visible, it was dark again. I knew that I'd be able to make it to the Order before everyone retired for the night, but was I ready to see everyone? To see Niamh? I sighed and let the unsteadiness of it decide for me.

I found a nice spot under the stars near a river and just out of sight of the main road. My pack fell to the ground with a loud thunk and I tried to not collapse next to it. I did everything I could to resist going to bed, knowing that I would be haunted by nightmares. Eventually my legs gave out, and I laid down, staring up at the sky. I let the slow bubbling of the river, and the twinkling of the all-seeing stars persuade me into an uneasy sleep. Only two things were constant, death and the unreachable stars. Did that mean that the five of them were watching over me from above? Rather than feeling uneasy, that thought soothed my heart.

As anticipated, my sleep was uneasy, and I found myself waking up with a scream on my lips multiple times during the night. When the sun began to inch upwards, I gave up on sleep and stretched, feeling every cut and bruise from the previous days, with nothing be more painful than the throbbing in the side of my head. "Can't delay this any longer," I whispered as I shouldered my pack and began the too-short walk. The forest, once something I considered a friend, became unfamiliar. I flinched at every sound around me, unused to how my left side would now be perceiving sound. Everything rang awkwardly in my head and the dissonance sent me collapsing to the ground multiple times only for me to scramble away from the way the forest ground crunched beneath me. It was only the vision of Niamh's worried face that had me rising again and beginning my unsteady way back home.

Chapter Three — Lysandra

"The nature of the Fae was wild, like the elements they controlled, and full of whimsy. Human nature is opposite to this. We thrive off stability and long for logic and reason. These natures are at constant war inside necromancers. When presented with outside factors, such as death, the clash results in the madness that all necromancers are infected with."

—Braekios Journal #2, page 3

I arrived in Braeton and everything was the same. The passersby smiled, merchants cheerily shouted advertisements, and a jaunty song came from a musician somewhere. Nothing changed. Nothing changed despite the five of them being gone. I kept my eyes down, doing my best not to draw attention but I felt their eyes on me; it would be hard to ignore a person with a bloody head and a large bag that clinked with every step.

I went straight to the Preceptor, fearing that I would lose courage if I stopped at my apartment first. My feet took me past places that would now always be haunted. Here was where Dinah, Niamh and I would sneak under the tables and make rat noises to scare the teachers away from their desserts. Outside that window was the tree where we carved our initials after one particularly bad fight about who would be making breakfast the next day. There were the stairs where we first found our "secret spot" on the roof that led to endless conversations, morning, day, and night.

My classmates called my name, and I heard gasps at my appearance as I continued to walk, but I ignored them and found myself in the Preceptor's office flanked by Mr. Rah and Mr. Jasper.

"Preceptor, I am here to report about Qui," I said formally, hoping the stiffness of it would prevent my voice from wobbling. I stood at parade rest in front of the Preceptor who hunched over his desk peering at a document. "Upon arrival we found the city people dead." I brought my hand to my head in confusion and amended, "Sorry, all except six were found dead. We tracked the necromancer to the Braeton-Daetopolis split. The necromancer was engaged, and we discovered the remaining six deceased residents. The necromancer was slain, by my hand, but the other five died during that fight." I'd honor Xavier's last wish; they didn't need to know that his death was self-inflicted. "I'm sorry, Preceptor, teachers. I tried my best, we all did." I didn't notice that I was crying until Mr. Jasper dabbed a tissue to the corner of my right eye.

The Preceptor placed one of his bone white hands on mine saying, "My dear, what happened was due to no fault of yours or the others. Life can be unnecessarily and unexpectedly cruel. I know your heart will be heavy for a long time, but as you walk around the city, look at the people around you and know that the smiles remain on their faces because of your bravery and the sacrifices of the others." He smiled faintly and his tenderness caused me to cry harder. "Go down to the sick bay and remain there until you are cleared to return to your normal schedule."

My bag was lifted off my aching shoulders and I was gently guided to the medical wing. I heard the teacher scold anyone who tried to approach but it sounded far away. I ended up in a soft bed with fresh gauze wrapped around my head and a slightly cool breeze coming from the open window above my head. With nothing better to do, and with no one to stop me, I slept.

And slept. I felt no hunger and traveled to and from the bathroom in a haze. My soul needed time to prepare for my new normal without Dinah, and I was more than happy to succumb to the welcoming nothingness that claimed me.

I woke again, with no idea of how much time had passed, to see Niamh's heart shaped face and black hair resting on my abdomen, her hand nearly touching mine. She raised her head when she felt my hand twitch, eyes flicking first to my missing left ear and then to my soulless eyes. They say the eyes are the windows to the soul. I wondered what she saw. Was my soul as shriveled and gray as I felt?

"I'm so glad you're back. It's been weeks since you first got here," she said, her brown eyes slightly watery and her smile trembling.

I tried to take a deep breath, but choked on the emotion seeing her brought up, and I cried, Niamh not far behind me. She scooted further on the bed and soon we sobbed into each other's arms. The only sound heard in the sick bay was our crying and occasional sniffles. When I was finally able to take a steadying breath, I told her everything.

She stayed silent until the very end and only said in a hard voice I had never heard her use before. "Good riddance. I'm glad you culled that monster."

I nodded, incapable of saying anything else before remembering Dinah's dagger.

"She'd want you to have it," I said, wondering if it ended up back with the weapons master, getting the cleaning and care it deserved.

Niamh thought for a second and then shook her head, that trembling smile back on her face. "You need to take it. Let her dagger remind you of what others can lose, what I can lose, if you're not careful."

We spoke well into the night, only stopping when our sentences began to be interrupted by yawns.

"You're getting released tomorrow?" She asked, rising to her feet.

"Yeah," I said, repressing a yawn.

It had been two weeks and the medic said that my wounds were healed enough, though I was told to take it easy for a little while.

"Great! Come find me once you do!" Were Niamh's parting words as she left.

With her gone I settled back down into my bed, wondering what the Order would be like without Dinah. I wrote a note and fell back asleep, this time determined to get out of bed the next morning. The next day I rose, dropped off the note on Niamh's nightstand letting her know that there was something that I needed to do before I could resume my normal life. My last stop before leaving was to the weapons master to get Dinah's dagger.

I walked all day, enjoying the little things like the breeze rustling my hair, the sound of twigs snapping below my feet, and the way my head was beginning to feel clear once again. I stopped for a brief meal by the river I camped out by on the way back, letting the water rush past my feet before walking again. The sun began to set once more when I finally made it back to the spot where my world had changed. The five of them were nothing more than ashes now and the wind carried them away. As I sat against a tree and took out Dinah's dagger, a tear fell, and I finally let myself mourn my best friend. No more, I wouldn't let there be any more death among those close to me. Five times I made this vow, and with each time, I cut one of the fingertips on my right hand. I made a vow that my blood would be the last human blood this ground soaked up. I spent the night there, reflecting on my time with all of them and letting the loss become a stone in my heart. I felt my life settle around that grief and I knew that while the pain would always be with me, that I would grow around it.

The next day, Niamh sat on the stairs to the Order to greet me. "Okay?" She asked, and as I responded, "Okay," I knew that while it wasn't the truth now, it would be one day.

It's been four years and twenty missions since then and something… Odd is going on. The necromancers are getting stronger, their power able to influence bodies from a greater distance and more decayed than normal.

My last mission almost ended the same as all the others, another pitiful necromancer (this one in the form of an older woman) begging me for its life. It was what it chose for its last words that gave me pause. "Nectar," it said, staring past me at something in the distance. "I wish I could have drunk Nectar one more time." I mulled over what the fuck Nectar could be as I travelled back to the Order on the back of a wagon occupied by a family travelling to the city. The youngest son asked constant questions about my lack of ear, the hatchet that hung at my side, and my clothes. I would have yelled at him if Nectar didn't pose as a puzzle for me to try to solve.

When I reported back to the Preceptor, he let out a massive sigh, saying nothing for a few minutes. He got up and beckoned me to follow him. I trailed him as he gathered all who were currently in the building.

"For a while we've been noticing a trend. Our enemy is getting stronger and there seems to be one commonality." He gave out a hacking cough before continuing. "Many of you have brought back reports containing the word Nectar. After interviewing multiple necromancers we have acquired, we believe this to be a substance, most likely an unnatural one, that can enhance their abilities. It does come with a price. It is incredibly addictive and necromancers will do anything in their power to procure it. We can use this all to our advantage, so we need to gather as much information on Nectar as possible. As of right now, this is the only lead we have, so please be vigilant as you go forth."

So here I am, wandering around this sunny little town, hoping to find the necromancer and learn whatever they know about Nectar. Though I doubted I'd find anything here, this town showed no signs of a recent necromantic attack. I casually walked over to a couple sitting on the edge of a dried-up fountain and tried to strike up a conversation. Before I could even state my purpose, they both shook their heads and walked away, the woman with a noticeable limp and a wounded foot. Okay, that was rude, but I understood being wary of strangers. I tried a different approach and went over to a teenage boy who was tying a shoe worn out so badly that I could see his swollen blue toes.

"Hi!" I said with a cheesy and cheery a smile as I could manage. "My mom and I moved in down the street, and I was wondering if you knew—" He opened his mouth to show me his lack of tongue before ambling off.

I was starting to get annoyed. I looked for the one type of person whose curiosity tended to outweigh common sense. My eyes caught on a young boy peering at me from around a corner. I pulled out Dinah's dagger and flipped it in the air, picking up speed as I slowly walked towards him. The boy was so entranced by my display that he didn't notice me until I was standing right in front of him. His one good eye, the other completely scarred over, widened as I knelt in front of him.

"Cool, right?" I asked softly. "I learned it while growing up in the Order. Have you heard of the Order?"

I was slow to realize that it wasn't me he stared at, but rather the crowd who had silently formed behind me. Slowly, I stood up and raised my hands in the universal, "I'm not a threat, please don't fuck me up" sign and said flatly, "I'm from the Order. I was sent here to help." Still not a word from the unmoving crowd. All their heads were cocked at the same angle to the left and their eyes seemed larger than they were in a way that made me feel small. They all stared at me with the same intensity, and I squirmed, my gut telling me something weird was going on. No, wait, it wasn't as if they seemed not to be blinking, they weren't blinking. I looked closer, no fingers twitched, no foot tapped the ground; they were completely still. "Still as the grave," was the last thing that passed through my mind before something hard hit the back of my head. I heard a soft chuckle that sent warm air down the back of my neck before everything went black.

Chapter Four — Talia

"Humans serve as the perfect prey for necromancers. We crave socialization and live in units that learn to survive together. Although we can be cruel to each other, when faced with a necromantic attack, humans will cast aside feuds to fight the greater evil. It is for this reason that necromancers will always seek to destroy human lives."

—Braekios Journal #5, page 1

I never knew my father, but I never wanted to. I had my mother, and my curiosity, and that was all I needed. We moved around a lot, Mom always saying that the wind told her of enchanting lands just a wagon ride away. To me, it seemed like we were running away, though I never knew from what. We'd pack up the few things we owned and would be on the next wagon out of town. We'd ride with anyone who was passing through, sometimes with a merchant, other times with a family leaving for a trip. Mom never picked a destination, stating that she would know home when she saw it. I was happy not to be left behind and loved the sense of whimsy I felt as we traveled through fields of flowers, across babbling rivers or dark and mossy forests. As soon as we arrived at the new city, town or village, Mom would quickly pick up jobs cleaning houses of those wealthy enough to afford not to do it themselves. Our house was usually an abandoned one provided to us in trade for Mom's services or rented from someone willing to accept the little money we could offer. I was left alone while she was working and occupied myself by wandering around my new temporary home. I tried to make friends, but we never stayed in one place long enough for me to form those bonds. Every place we went to had different flowers and I quickly developed a fascination for gardening. If we had a spare room, Mom would let me convert it into a tiny greenhouse where I was able to care for my plants to my heart's content, otherwise I created a small garden behind our house and fended off anything that looked to eat my precious sprouts.

We arrived in Exela when I was ten, and although Mom said it was just another place to rest briefly, I desperately wanted to stay. Exela was small, smaller than any of the other places we lived in, but wealthy. The road had cobblestones that were cleaned regularly and a small school where the children were sent to learn to read and write, something that many of the other towns we lived in didn't have. Most of the adults in this town were scholars of some kind and made their living by selling new designs and gadgets, relying on merchants to buy their wares in bulk to distribute across the continent.

Merchants would visit regularly to purchase the latest creations, like some kind of new tinted glasses to help people work in the overly bright sun, or a new salve that could help with certain skin diseases. Every fourth day of the week the town came together to form the marketplace and people traded knowledge, gossip, and their wares. Children would run around attempting to sneak food and listen to stories getting told by the town's only entertainer. During the summer, people would gather down by the lake and spend all day on blankets sharing food, watching the kids play or swim, and washing clothes. The winter months smelled of faint woodsmoke as fires lit all the homes and the taverns where someone could get a warm cup of tea and a rich soup. I loved all Exela's seasons, mild enough to be enjoyable but also still would experience the nip of frost and the occasional snowfall. Spring was my favorite though. When the weather warmed up, the bulbs that slumbered during the winter sprung through the tough ground in bursts of red, pinks and yellows. The grass around the lake was littered with little wildflowers that the younger kids would weave into crowns to be sold for a copper piece each. All my time would be spent outside by the lake, from the second the sun rose to when the sun set, I could be found watering the plants, or simply laying among the flowers making shapes out of the clouds.

I loved Exela, loved the way you could feel life happening around you, but despite calling Exela home for longer than the other places we lived, I never made any friends. I was an outsider to the kids my age, my hair blonde in a town of auburn, skin tanned from spending most of my time outside compared to the pale scholars and students that lived and flocked to Exela. Our home sat outside town, on the hill above the lake, and we were far enough away that we didn't get visitors. It was old and in need of repair, but sturdy. The kitchen was centered around the fireplace and was just big enough to fit a small table and two chairs. To the left was the one bedroom that Mom and I shared, her sleeping on the small cot and I curled up on a pile of blankets on the stony floor. I didn't mind it during the summer as it kept me cool, but the winters could be harsh and sometimes I spent the entire night shivering, unable to get warm despite being cocooned in the blankets. The best part of the house, though, was the view. There was a door in the bedroom that had a large window in it. Through it, I had a breathtaking view of the lake, and I liked nothing more than throwing it open first thing in the morning to soak in the sun of a new day.

One of Mom's clients was Imogene, the tutor that worked at the school, and I was fascinated by her. Her long copper hair always shone like freshly polished brass, and she had a kind smile for anyone who spoke to her. I was also entranced by the overcoat she always wore. It fell to her knees and was a dark shade of purple that reminded me of sunsets. It also had pockets that seemed to be endlessly deep and were always bulging with contents that I always wondered about. Anyone under the age of thirteen was equally enthralled by her and we all would crowd around her, hoping she'd fish out a treat for us from one of those wonderful

pockets.

I was envious of those kids, they got to spend time with her inside the classroom and I

was left to stand outside wondering what kind of incredible things they were learning. I once

asked Mom if I could attend school, pointing out that I was the only one who didn't go, to be told

that I wasn't like the other children and didn't need an education.

"Look at me," she said, gesturing to our house. "Look at where we are. I've always been

able to take care of us, providing us with food, a house and clothing. I never received an

education and if I didn't need one, you don't either." The punishment I received after was swift

and brutal, so I tended to leave that topic alone.

But, after one particularly bad day, I felt lonely and incredibly irritated due to Lani, one

of the students, calling me an ignorant slug after catching me trying to peer through the window.

"Please Mom," I begged. "If I could read and write I could earn some money. I asked Mr.

Twill if he would be willing to let me read his mail and transcribe his response since he can't see

very well, and he said yes." I hoped that logic and the idea of money would win her over, but I

was wrong.

"No," she said sternly, not bothering to look away from the pot she stirred that rested

over the coals.

I stomped my foot, whining. "It's not fair! Ms. Imogene teaches all the kids, and she said

she'd be willing to let me attend for free!"

She stopped stirring briefly at this, only to say, "We all must earn our way in this life.

We will not accept charity from anyone no matter how badly you may want it. I've told you

before. Those skills will have you locked away in a dusty room, when you could be learning real skills like cooking or carpentry. Look at me, I can both read and write and yet that isn't how I feed us. You can't earn money by reading a book like you can from selling clothes that you have sewn or the food you made. Now I've already said no, so go and wash up."

Being eleven, I didn't like hearing no, so I reacted the only way I knew would get her attention, by screaming and yanking the spoon from her hand. I wanted her to look at me and see this was more than just wanting to go to school. I was lonely and desperately wanted to feel like I belonged somewhere. Instead of grabbing the spoon, I knocked over the pot, spilling our meager dinner of vegetables and rabbit into the coals. She did look at me then, her eyes flashing with anger, and I could tell by the way she clenched her hands that I'd severely miscalculated her calm.

"If you want to eat tonight, I suggest digging out your dinner before it gets too burnt, because I will not be feeding you." She spoke no more after that and walked out the door, my apologies falling on stone ears.

I was able to get a small piece of rabbit and a single carrot out of the coals before the burns on my hands became too painful. My stomach still rumbled but I curled up in my blankets, hoping that sleep would ease the sting in my hands and the stabs of hunger in my stomach. I slept with my hands in my mouth that night, willing my saliva to cool my burnt fingers.

Morning came, and Mom still hadn't returned home, so I went out looking for her, intending to apologize and grovel if that was what it took for us to move past the argument. I checked all the places she could normally be found at, avoiding the groups of people milling about, but didn't find her anywhere. The last house I checked was Imogene's. I knocked and waited only a few seconds before turning back, planning on waiting for Mom at our house. As I began to leave, the door opened, and Imogene took one look at the blisters on my hands before

ushering me inside.

"Is Kattia here?" I asked awkwardly, standing inside and looking around the large house

she lived in. I let out a sigh of defeat at Imogene's head shake and slumped down the wall to sit

on the floor.

"I'm sorry, sweet girl, but I haven't seen your mom since she was here yesterday."

I placed my hands on the cold stones and hissed when the action brought on pain instead

of relief. Imogene knelt and gently picked up my hands, turning them over to examine them.

"When did you burn yourself?" She asked, looking closer at my wounds.

I mumbled, "Yesterday," too embarrassed of my childish outburst to tell her the full

story.

Nodding, she stood up and pulled me to my feet. With one of my wrists in her hands, she

guided me down the hall saying, "Come. I have something that can help with the pain."

The room we entered smelled earthy like wet soil and slightly floral, with a giant wooden

table in the middle and small desk tucked in the corner. I couldn't help but stare at the desk as it

seemed to be fighting for space with a large drying rack full of flowers, herbs, and other plants.

Given that I couldn't see the wall through everything that hung upside down to dry, I'd say that

the desk was losing the battle. There were books stacked unevenly in one corner and I had to

crane my neck to see the top tome. The sun that came in through the large window behind me

reflected off something and I turned to see the shelves containing hundreds of little and big jars

full of different liquids and crushed up plants. I knew without a doubt that no matter what I saw

in my life, this room would remain one of the most magical places I came across. I felt the

exuberance of life etched in every inch of space in the room. There was a sense of well-being and peace that immediately put me at ease, and I paused to take it all in. It was the books, though, that held my attention. I couldn't help but wonder what secrets they might hold.

Seeing where my gaze landed, Imogene smiled. "I'm not a university-trained medic, but I like to believe that the knowledge I've acquired can be helpful. Now, sit on this table while I find what I need."

She helped me hop onto the table and I watched her rummage among the plants, moving some away to peer deeper into their depths.

"Aha!" She said, bringing over two different plants and grabbing a nearby mortar and pestle.

She spoke while grinding them up, adding more into the mortar slowly. "There are many plants that contain nutrients and other elements that can be beneficial to humans. Some, when combined properly, can help with different types of pain. This one," she held up a thick leaf, "can only be found during the summer, when the sun is at its brightest. It soothes burns such as yours. This one," she held up the second, a stem with multiple small yellow flowers, "I grow in my garden. It will help make sure that your hands don't get infected."

She ground them into a thick paste and rubbed it gently on my hands. I closed my eyes at the almost instant relief I felt. Imogene pulled a small tin container off the shelf and scooped the remaining mixture into it. She set it down next to me. "Take this with you. If your hands start to hurt again, rub a small amount across the burnt area and it will dull the pain." She watched me for a few seconds, studying the way I mutely followed her instructions before saying quietly, "You know, all these books are about plants, living things and all the wonderful things they can do. I've seen you down by the lake, tending to the plants around it, wouldn't you like to know more about them? If you'd like, you can borrow any book if you return it."

She frowned as I said, "That's very nice of you, but I don't know how to read. My mom won't let me go to school."

A tear made its way down my face despite my best efforts not to cry.

She came over and wiped it away, before whispering in my ear, "We must not let her know then."

The idea of hiding something from my mom terrified me, but I longed to be literate and have something to do during the long summer days, so I agreed. We arranged for our first session, and I returned home, skipping the entire way, the reason for my trip into town pushed aside by the thrill of starting my lessons. That is until I saw Mom putting food onto the table. At the sound of the door creaking open she turned and almost dropped the plate of food in her haste to reach me. She pulled me in for a suffocating hug and I clung to her, hoping she couldn't sense my betrayal.

Pressing kisses to my head, she apologized. "I'm so sorry, little one. I knew it was an accident, but I was so angry, I was afraid of what I would've done if I stayed home. I went to a friend's house in town and lost track of time."

"I'm sorry too, Mom," my words spoken into the warmth of her embrace, and I tried to soothe my unease at going behind her back by trying to apologize for what she didn't know. "I didn't mean to get upset; I just want the other kids to like me."

She didn't respond except to go bring something from the other room, and I saw something small and black that wriggled in her arms, eager to escape.

"I know you're lonely, but you're so much better off without having those kids in your life. I brought you a new friend. Someone who won't leave and who will always want to play."

Opening her arms, a little black kitten poked its head out and mewed. I took him in my arms and brought him up to my face to look at him better. We stared at each other for a minute before he purred and licked my nose. I giggled, delighted to finally have someone to love me.

"He's missing a leg, so he won't be able to run after you very well, but when I saw how sweet he was, I knew that you'd love him regardless of his flaws."

"He's perfect, Mom!" I gave her a one-armed hug, doing my best not to squeeze the kitten as well.

I set him down to explore and we watched, trying to come up with a good name. When he bumped into the side of the table and ran from the cup of water that fell because of it, we laughed and decided to call him Trickster. Trickster became my almost constant companion and followed me everywhere. The one place I forbade him from joining me was into town, I knew how the kids treated things that weren't the same as them and I worried what they'd do to him.

I began my lessons with Imogene, tracing the shapes she drew in the sand by the beach, as she explained that these symbols were letters and made up all the sounds we used in our language. "Mom," I'd call into the house, hoping for no response before I'd clear away my blankets and squat on the ground to write imaginary letters, teaching Trickster everything I learned. I was obsessed, and refused to stop, choosing to strain my eyes in the dying light rather than entertain myself with something else. It was only the creak of the front door that had me rushing to open the door and greet mom, hoping she couldn't see the guilt on my face. Every night my dreams were filled with words. My days soon fell into a comfortable routine, with morning reading lessons, and the afternoons finding me trekking around the lake trying to identify the plants and write their names. Trickster was always there, chasing a butterfly or rolling through the grass and basking in the sun.

Chapter Five — Talia

"Necromancers aren't born, they are created from trauma. A child can appear human for most of its life until it is forced to recognize the power that lays within it. It is at that moment, that the eyes will change from whatever color it was at birth to the unnatural shades that are unique only to necromancers."

—Braekios Journal #2, page 23

I turned fifteen in Exela, the first time I ever celebrated more than one birthday in the same place. I didn't have a big celebration like those in town who would throw a large party and invite all the townspeople, but I did receive two wonderful gifts. The first was from Mom—a long emerald jacket with pockets deep enough to hold whatever I wanted. I knew that it cost her at least a month's wages and I was grateful that she'd listened to my complaints about never having enough hands to carry stuff to make this for me. I also knew that I would cherish the jacket for as long as I lived. The second gift was a small leather-bound book from Imogene.

"Now you can write down everything you know about those plan
ts you care for. Maybe one day, when I'm gone, you can use it to help people," she said as she gave it to me.

I took it with me everywhere I went, writing down anything and everything in my most careful handwriting. I kept the book hidden under a loose floorboard below my bed so that Mom wouldn't find it.

One summer day not long after my birthday, I rushed into town to meet with Imogene, and it wasn't until I heard the kids jeer, "Look at that thing! What a freak of nature, it can't even walk right!" That I realized Trickster had followed me. I was already running late and eager to use every second of my time with Imogene that I'd forgotten to tie Trickster up outside like I normally did.

I turned to see the kids surrounding Trickster and taking turns lunging towards him, making him cower. I tried to push my way through but after a quick gesture from Lani, two large boys who served as her goons grabbed my arms and used their height to force me to the ground and watch as Trickster recoiled from the kicks, mewing pathetically. I tried to pull free, but their hands only tightened. Lani laughed cruelly at Trickster's meows and lunged forward, landing on Trickster's tail, and he gave out a pained screech. Emboldened by her actions, Timsen, a pimply boy, grabbed Trickster by his tail. Terian pulled Trickster towards him, and I heard Trickster's claws scrape against the cobblestones, trying to find traction and failing. Timsen used his palm to force Trickster to the ground, making his legs splay out around himself. Dahlia and Natalie, twins who were my nearest neighbors and never apart, held him down, pulling his legs out in opposite directions so Trickster couldn't get away.

"Do it, Timsen! Let's see if it looks better with a missing tail to match that missing leg!" Lani stood a few steps away, hands on her hips, a sneer upon her face as she surveyed the scene.

Stomp after stomp, Trickster cried out in pain, and the way his eyes stared at me in agony had my throat growing hoarse with my screams. I looked to see if any of the adults had noticed something going on, but everyone that looked my way quickly looked away, writing it off as kids being kids. Trickster's screams eventually stopped, and the kids shrugged before walking off, talking about what they were going to do next. I crawled my way to Trickster and gently scooped up his mangled body, holding him close to me. I couldn't feel a heartbeat and the stillness of his form had me sprinting home, cradling him close to my chest.

"Mom! Help! Trickster needs help!"

Mom turned towards me as soon as she heard me throw open the door. I hoped she'd run over and take control of the situation, assuring me that Trickster would be okay, rather she walked over and slowly lowered me and Trickster to the floor, a sympathetic smile on her face.

"I'm sorry, little one, but Trickster is gone. There isn't anything we can do."

"No!" I refused to accept it without trying anything first. I scrambled towards the bandages we kept in the bathroom in case of injuries, one hand still holding onto Trickster while I used the other to crawl across the ground, but stopped when Mom's hand gently squeezed my arm. Tears gathered in my eyes, and I swiped at my face, turning it red from Trickster's blood. "He can't be gone! I love him! He can't leave me! He can't!"

On my knees I rocked Trickster over and over, my tears soaking his soft black fur. In the back of my mind I heard a faint mewing, distant, but I was confident it belonged to Trickster despite his vocal cords having been crushed during the assault. My eyes closed and through the darkness of my mind I chased after that sound, until it was a roar. The mew was loud enough to make me wince and I flinched away from it.

Then it was gone and the only thing I heard was Mom whispering a quivering, "No, please."

My eyes opened slowly, and Mom's horrified look aimed at Trickster confused me. Looking down, I saw why she looked so panicked. Trickster wasn't moving much, but his tail started to twitch in the way only living felines do. I brought Trickster to my face to assure myself that he was okay, but Mom wrenched my head to face her, staring deep into my eyes, and I saw her own eyes go wide in fear at whatever she saw in them.

"No. No, no, no," she repeated, letting me go and crawling backwards to the wall, putting as much distance between us as you could in this small house.

"Mom, you're scaring me, what's wrong?"

She tensed as I walked over to her. I reached out to touch her and reassure myself that everything was okay but pulled my hand back when she flinched. She saw my frown and gave a gentle pat on my leg. It was obvious she was trying to be reassuring but the way only her fingertips touched me told me something was very wrong.

"Nothing is wrong, dear," she said, straining to make her voice light. "Go and wash up for dinner."

She got up and walked to the meat that was starting to burn. It was quiet in the house that night, except for Trickster's purring. He didn't leave my side, and as we ate dinner, I frequently reached down to run a hand over his coat, reassuring myself that he was alive although his lack of breathing worried me. I pushed the thought out of my mind, writing it off as the shock of the events causing the details, like his breath, to slip my mind.

"Good night, little one," Mom said before walking into town, claiming that she was going to have a drink with a friend. There was no goodbye hug or kiss on my head, and I fell asleep that night with a knot in my stomach.

When I woke the next morning, she wasn't home, but I tried to push away the knot that remained and hoped for another normal day. I went into town to beg Imogene for a quick lesson on mathematics, only to find her teaching, and unavailable for the rest of the day. Determined to still learn something today, I decided to go down to the lake and practice by myself, but found my focus caught on the reflection across the water, the way the grass felt beneath my feet, or the song that echoed in my head. I passed the time laying on the grass, humming along to a rhythm that I knew couldn't be heard by others and giggling at the absurdity of it all.

Eventually, the rumbling of my stomach had me getting to my feet and skipping home for a meal. Mom still wasn't home, but there were signs that she'd returned while I was gone; her clothes and other things were missing, as well as some of the nonperishable food. A closer look showed that she also left something behind. I approached the table and saw a pair of tinted lenses surrounded by gold frames, and a letter.

The glasses were like the ones created in Exela but were noticeably darker than the ones sold in town, so dark my eyes would be fully hidden behind them. I examined them for a bit before setting them down and reaching for the letter, not thinking anything of it. It wasn't until after I read the first line—

"Dear Talia, I know you can read this, because I've seen you practicing your letters."

—that I knew I was caught. I should've felt fear, or dread at being discovered, but my chest felt full of butterflies, and the idea of being punished when Mom returned was comical. I didn't question why Mom didn't confront me, choosing to examine the quality of the paper and how graceful Mom's handwriting was.

"Before I begin, I need you to look at your reflection in our looking glass and understand that your life is about to be forever changed."

My hunger forgotten; dread turned my body cold. I brought the letter with me into the bathroom and looked in the glass. I let out a small scream and brought my fingers to the eyes of my reflection before touching my own, hoping that what I was seeing wasn't right. I was used to seeing brown eyes looking back at me, but now silver eyes stared at me in horror. I sank to the floor and gulped down air as Trickster came over to curl up in my lap, sensing my distress. Tears turned my vision blurry for several long minutes, my sobbing drowning out the comforting sound of Trickster's purring. Once my world came back into focus, I returned to the letter,

"As all know, a necromancer can be identified by three things: the dead they raise, the madness that follows, and their unnatural eyes. While I hope that the madness will spare you, there's no evidence that you won't be taken by it. I left, sparing us the chance of my death at your hands."

I laughed, the sound bouncing off the bare walls, at the joy I felt knowing that I could create my own friends and force the dead to stay by my side for as long as I wanted them to.

"Well Trickster," I rested my head against the wall, "Do you think I'm mad?" He said nothing. "Hmm, if this is madness, I think I'm okay with it."

I continued to read. *"But I cannot leave you in the dark of your origins. Your father was not the man I thought he was. I was a country girl and he won me over with gifts brought from exotic places and promises of taking me to travel the world. He charmed me, with his dazzling smile and sweet words. We fell in love and had a happy life for the first few months. Slowly, he took over my life. I had to ask permission to go into town, only cook meals from his approved list, and wasn't allowed to have anyone over. My own mother and father, who lived in the town over the hill, were refused entry when they came to see me for my birthday. "There's sickness that's spreading, I don't want to risk us," he said, and I believed him. I thought it was because he cared about me and didn't want harm to come to me, but I soon learned that he was protecting himself. When I was pregnant with you, I watched as a tree bent down and extended its limbs for him to cut and shape into the crib you'd sleep in. There was no denying what type of monster he was: Fae. I knew that I had to escape, so I swallowed the scream that rested behind my teeth and cooed at him when he presented me with that cursed crib. While he was sleeping that night, I used an iron pole pulled from the well out back to pin him to the bed and force the truth from him. His lips pulled up in an inhuman snarl as he told me the truth. Althorian Ostyx was his name, and he served as a General in the war long ago. In the final days of war, he knew his kind had lost and he was determined to survive. There was no chance he wouldn't be hunted if people knew what he really was, so he disguised himself. He cut the tell-tale tips off his ears, used his magic to change the color of his eyes from their natural red to a muddy brown, found a small town far away from the battlefield, and began his life again. After a few years, he grew bored, and wanted a plaything, so he found a human wife: me."*

"When he found out that I was with child, he was determined to raise that child as Fae and use its abilities to reignite the old conflict and regain what was lost. I already belonged to him, body and soul, I refused to let him own you, too. I didn't need to hear anymore; I forced a sleeping draught I had bought through his lips and ran away. I ran, never stopping, terrified that he'd find me, find us, and force us into a war that we didn't want to be in. The best and worst day of my life was when I gave birth to you. I lived in fear of what I would see in your eyes, but when they opened and were a human brown, I had thought we would be fine, that you had escaped your father's curse. I was wrong, and although I've enjoyed all the time we had, I know that we'll never be able to go back to what it was like before. If you cared for the humanity you used to pretend to be a part of, you would end your life once you finished reading this letter, but you're young and naive and I imagine you won't be able to make the most important choice of your life. I've left you with some special glasses that will hide your eyes. The townspeople wear them during the day so you won't seem suspicious, but if your father couldn't hide himself, I doubt you will be able to. Nonetheless, you were my daughter, and I wish you luck in your life. May it be short and painless. Goodbye, little one."

There was nothing else in the letter. I didn't know what to do next, but I refused to become a tool of my father's and refused to be haunted by my mom's disgust. Something made its way to the front of my mind. I focused and the sensation became clearer. It was the feeling of a gentle hand brushing against soft fur.

"Is that you, Trickster?" I pet him, and when I pet him, he purred louder. I had nothing but time on my hands, so I guessed I'd learn what it means to be a necromancer.

I don't know how much time passed, just that I spent most of it inside my head, listening to Trickster and learning how to interact with the voice in my head. There was a knock at the door that pulled me from my contemplation, and when I didn't open it, Imogene heaved it open and came to stand in front of me.

"What's wrong, Talia?" She asked when I looked away from her and didn't rise from the floor where I sat.

"Mom is gone. Go-one," I sang, assuming that this was the madness that Mom wrote about. I should have been anxious about the reaction I'd receive when Imogene learned the truth, but all I felt was the joy of not being alone for once in my life. I had Trickster with me, now and always, and with his little voice inside my head I would never need to talk to anyone ever again. Why should I have cared if the person I loved almost as much as my cat deserted me, or if the only other person who made me feel like I belonged flinched away when she learned the truth, when I could now make people be my friend? "I'm a necromancer and she's gone." I did laugh then, loud and aloof. It felt good, to make a sound out loud after communicating silently, and I laughed for long minutes, stopping only when my throat grew pained, and the laughter turned into a squeak.

I looked at Imogene, expecting her to run out of the house, potentially while screaming. Instead, her mouth dropped, her eyes widened in surprise, but her hands remained and rubbed at the tears I hadn't realized fell. She pulled me into a hug that warmed me and pulled me from the dark place I'd fallen into. I let myself remain there, hoping to borrow her strength and faith in me.

"I have no idea how your monster of a mother would expect you to harm her when you've never harmed anyone in your time here. Come live with me, my house has plenty of empty rooms and spots for you to make your own."

"I hear him, Imogene. I hear Trickster. What if I kill you because Trickster told me to do it?"

She smiled. "While I doubt Trickster wants me dead, if he all of a sudden changes his mind, we'll deal with it. Just because you can hear their voices doesn't mean that you need to listen. You'll need to learn when to heed them and when to tune them out. You should be the one giving out the orders, not them. We can do this together, Talia; you won't be alone anymore. What do you say, want to come live with me?"

She didn't wait for my answer, just pulled me to my feet and looked around. "What should we take with us?"

I grabbed the green jacket, herbology notebook and Trickster. I slid the glasses onto my face and left the house for the last time. I had no need to look back and remind myself of the painful past, everything I needed was ahead of me and in my arms.

Chapter Six — Talia

"Necromancers are drawn to death and need it to live, much like humans need water to survive. Death is irresistible to a necromancer and when near it, they feel the pull of the dead. No necromancer can resist resurrecting the dead around them regardless of if it was human or animal. To limit their chaos, we must burn any living matter including deceased family, pets, and livestock. It is inhuman to allow the deceased to be manipulated instead of residing in their eternal rest."

—Braekios Journal #6 , page 55

Imogene kept me busy, and my time was spent filling my insatiable need for knowledge. We continued with my literacy, building beyond numbers and words to include science of the body and advanced medicine. I refused to leave our home, terrified that I'd raise a corpse and be burned for my actions. I'd grown used to the sound of Trickster's voice in my head. The madness lessened, and there were only a few, rare occasions when I gave into the impulses it put in my head, like chasing down a mouse I saw in the hallway or curling up in a sunbeam. After a month of coaxing, Imogene convinced me to leave our house and come with her into town, with the promise that she'd render me unconscious if I acted weird. When her services were requested, I'd trail after her, holding her supplies as I watched her set a bone, or stitch up a wound. At night I'd collapse into bed, Trickster curled up on me, and I'd dream of the day when I'd be able to help more than by holding her bag and medical things.

But you can't expect the past to be happy about being forgotten, and I learned this on one awful day. Imogene had gotten an urgent missive, begging her to come attend to one of the elders in town who'd fallen while walking down the stairs. We rushed through the town and into the bedroom where the old man lay, but it only took one look at his dazed expression and the pool of blood around his head to know that nothing could be done. Imogene quietly broke the news to the family, and we exited the house, their sobs following us out into the street.

"We stay," Imogene said when I questioned why we were still there despite knowing he would be dead soon. "To honor the family and him. We'll help the family prepare the body for the pyre and listen to their stories. Our bodies may burn, and our ashes spread to the winds, but our souls live on in our loved ones' hearts and minds."

As the family's cries reached a crescendo, I became aware of a deep baritone singing a wordless song inside my head.

"He sings," I whispered, and Imogene whipped her head from the window to my face, confusion growing.

"He sings, he sings, he sings," I chanted, this new voice was the only thing that mattered at this point. The words needed to escape me, and I needed to feel the voice embrace me.

I swayed to the rhythm of his song, and it warmed my body. Imogene's confusion switched to alarm.

"Talia?" She asked, grabbing me by the arm to stop me from going where I wanted to go most desperately, back inside the house where my new loyal friend laid. "Who sings? I don't hear anything."

I threw my head back, all the town needed to hear my exaltation, this wondrous experience. "He sings! Mathias sings and I must join him!"

I ripped myself free of Imogene's grasp and grabbed the doorknob, ready to see his smile and feel his warm embrace. But before I could be reunited with Mathias, Imogene pulled me back, fear turning her white, as she finally understood.

"Talia," she pleaded, pulling me back and into the nearest alley. "Mathias is dead, and we must return home."

Home was where Mathias was, and I needed to go home. I screamed, hoping that people would hear me and come to my aid, but no one did. Imogene wrapped one hand around my mouth and another around my waist as she dragged me through the alleyways back to our house. I only heard the song, which grew more and more urgent. Imogene managed to wrestle me through the house and the hallways and threw me into my room. She quickly propped the door closed with a heavy chair, and although I heard her slump to the ground with a sob, I was beyond caring.

Inside the room I twirled and danced, tasting the ecstasy of the song, which was distant but still present on my tongue, feeling the beat warm my body. Mathias and I were going to be forever intertwined, dancing, singing, and laughing together for all of eternity. I giggled, and it turned into a hysterical laugh that had my body folded in half until I collapsed onto the floor.

"Please Talia, let him go! You're not yourself right now. Please come back to me before I'm forced to hurt you," Imogene said from the other side of the door. The threat of pain by the hand of someone I cherished would normally have been enough to force me to be still, but Mathias promised me that we didn't need her, so I laughed at her idle threat. I was so entranced by the way the sun created little rays on the ground that I didn't hear the door creak open or feel the needle that pricked my neck.

"Talia, are you well?" She asked from the corner where she sat, noticing I stirred after taking the brief, unwilling nap.

I felt myself return to my body, and registered my stiff muscles, an intense headache, and a bone-deep chill.

"Imogene, I'm scared." While I was certain it was madness, it was at a level I was unused to, and it consumed me like a flame leaving no room beyond its burn inside my soul. I was sure I looked as shaken as I felt because she quickly pulled me in for a hug, and I tried to let her humanity fill me up.

"What happened?" I asked when I felt less shaken.

She sighed. "As soon as Mathias died, you started acting possessed and you ranted about a song. I managed to get you sedated, but not before the deceased's grandson came knocking on our door, teary-eyed and talking about how their supposedly dead grandfather sat up and looked around. I managed to get back to the house before the corpse left and convinced the family that it was an after-effect of death that can occur when a brain injury was the cause. They believed me and followed my advice of burning him sooner than they anticipated. I wouldn't be surprised if his 'song' ended as soon as his brain was burnt."

"I'm so sorry, Imogene." My apology felt inadequate, but I wasn't sure what else to say. I cried, feeling like the monster Mom said I was. Imogene let me cry, giving me the time I needed to confront the complete lack of control. My tears finally stopped, and I had the courage to ask, "What am I going to do?"

"Well," she said, determination lighting up her eyes. "What *we* are going to do is use all our apothecarial knowledge to create a suppressant. But I do have to ask, why now? You brought Trickster back months ago and you've never acted like that before. What was different with Mathias?"

I searched my mind for the soft sound of Trickster that was still with me and compared it with Mathias's voice. "I think it has to do with exposure and size. Trickster's a small cat, and I grew used to having his song in my head, it was easy to not let it overpower me. But Mathias was bigger and new, I was unprepared for the onslaught of his song. Where Trickster's is a whisper, Mathias's was a scream."

With that second brutal encounter out of the way, we began our research and were determined to help me in any way we could.

Nothing could pull me out of the house then. Not the slight breeze that tickled my neck coming in from the window, not Imogene's pleading, or Trickster's scratches at the front door. I refused to risk having another episode like the one I had with Mathias. I threw myself into our research, my eyes racing through every text we had in hopes of finding something we'd overlooked. I tried every combination of plants, insects, and other things like tree bark, and poured my hopes into it, so sure that this would be the one. I'd drink it, or slather it on my chest, or inject it into my blood and then wait. Imogene would bring something recently deceased, like a bird or a mouse, and I would hear their songs, low and underwhelming. With every attempt, I tried to not feel hopeful or let my heart tell me that this was the one that would work, but every time I still heard their little voices in my mind, I'd feel crushing defeat.

The only one who enjoyed these test sessions was Trickster, and he'd usually chase these creatures around until Imogene grew tired of watching and would kill them again. I'd force myself to smile and laugh but it never stopped the tears from falling when I was alone at night.

My eighteenth birthday was unremarkable for the most part, until my eyes snagged on something in a text that I'd probably already read a thousand times. I turned to Imogene who ground something up nearby.

"Imogene!" I couldn't help the excitement in my voice. "What about this?" I showed her a picture of a purple flower with a long stem, dotted in thorns that seemed to gleam with a wetness.

"Philipa's Prison," she squinted at the text. "There have been a few cases where those pricked claimed to have mind fog take over them and were incapable of following simple instructions."

Her eyes darted around as if reading an internal book until she finally said, "That might work! If we combine it with a stimulant like Ormortium, which workers use to help work later and faster, it might block the signals to your brain while allowing you to maintain control!" She frowned. "Or making your brain sleepy will let the song take control of you quicker and stronger. We'll need to be careful, Talia."

"Yeah, yeah, yeah, we'll never know until we try! Come on, Imogene, this might be it!" I already pushed her out the door and to our garden, eager to get the plants and get to work.

I felt something that I usually tried to squash, hope, however, this time felt different. This time I was optimistic, too. Something about the myth of Philipa's Prison, centered around a woman who created her own prison rather than let her father marry her off to someone she didn't love, struck a chord within me. It couldn't be mere coincidence that she and I both looked to escape something created by our bloodline.

Every step we did was meticulously measured and documented, on the off chance that this did work. We added water to help the poultice be ingested better. Imogene left to kill one of the rats we kept in a locked room for this exact purpose, and I drank the potion.

I didn't need to strain to hear the rat's little song to know that it worked. A soft thud had me swinging my head around to see that Trickster had collapsed to the floor. I ran over and knelt by him, praying for a twitch to let me know he was still with us, but there was nothing, no movement, and more importantly, his voice disappeared from my mind. It was hard to be happy about the tincture working when the other half of my soul lay unmoving.

"Well?" Imogene asked, walking back into the room, to find me on the floor close to tears. "I take it that means it worked? This is good, Talia. Why are you crying?"

"How could I not be? When Trickster is lying there, dead again." I brought his head to my face, and I nuzzled his soft fur.

"What if he's only dead for the moment?"

That caught my attention and I stopped to peer up at her. "What do you mean?"

"This is the first time your powers have been suppressed; we have no idea if you can resurrect him once they return. We'll need to wait and see. Tell me, how do you feel? How long did it take before it took effect?"

Imogene went right into research mode, and I didn't have the chance to wonder if she was right about Trickster as I told her about the experience. Once she was satisfied with my answers, she put away her notebook, letting me know that we'd need to be vigilant with our research.

"The next steps will include testing its potency." I could tell she was excited by this opportunity. "I hope you liked the way it tasted, because you're going to be drinking a lot of it."

The tincture wore off after four days, and much to my relief, I was able to bring forth Trickster's song again, although it was slightly more difficult, and it sounded as if his voice was slightly further away and less lively.

I tried explaining the feeling to Imogene. "When I raise something, I feel them connect to me. It's like their soul sings with mine. When I brought Trickster back this time, it felt like there was less of him with me."

"You'll need to pay attention to that. There may come a time when you won't be able to bring him back," was Imogene's response, and we began to limit my intake of it.

We expanded our tests, trying to determine what size group the tincture could suppress before the group was too large and I brought them back. We managed to do this with minimal problems except for one notable experience where the tincture failed to prevent me from reanimating a dozen birds, which resulted in Trickster being chased around the house by birds with a grudge while Imogene and I tried to re-kill them.

My knowledge and confidence in my gifts grew exponentially during that time and we wrote down everything, filling my notebook with our findings. I took the tincture which we called Philipa's Tincture frequently, and I carried several bottles of it with me everywhere I went. Trickster came back each time the tincture wore off, but his song continued to grow weaker, and I knew I didn't have much longer with him. There was a bit of a commotion when I was seen back in the village after being gone for so long, but once the townspeople had decided that I was not in fact a ghost, the gossip found a different topic.

The wet sickness came as it always did, but stronger than any of the previous times. We tried to isolate ourselves and prevent it from spreading, but our role as apothecaries meant we ventured into town whenever the illness found a new victim. When Imogene caught it, she sent me out in her place to help those who were sick. I drank Philipa's Tincture almost daily those few months as more and more people were taken before their time. Those months were dark, and I lived in a constant state of paranoia that the tincture would wear off. I tried to prepare for the deaths of the townspeople, but as time ticked by, I had to ration my doses, and soon I was only able to drink one as the last one wore off. The tincture would wear off and I would soon be overwhelmed by the recently deceased. Those were the scariest days, the ones where the madness took hold of me. Hours would be spent with me rolling on the floor naked, singing praise to the newest addition of my chorus, or staring at a wall until the tears soaked my clothes. During these days I was heavily sedated with Trickster for company Soon, the next one to die from it was Imogene, and I thanked the constellations above me that I was able to hold her hand as she passed. She made me promise to let her remain dead, but as I watched the flames eat at the one person I cherished, I wished I had her back with me, even if it was a false life.

Finally, the weather grew warm and dry, signaling the end of the wet sickness, and I was able to restock my supply of the tincture, though I needed it less as only the people who remained were the healthy ones who survived. The survivors walked around town tentatively, as if slightly afraid of this new normal, and I tried not to walk as if I was haunted by the memory of Imogene.

I continued to live in our house and turned half of the rooms into a small clinic where everyone was welcomed. I stayed busy, tending to anything from a scraped knee to a broken nose, and after a while I realized that I was happy. Sure, Imogene was gone, and Trickster spent most of his time curled up on a pillow in my room unmoving, but I had a purpose, and I used my skills to do something good.

Chapter Seven — Talia

"Necromancers can raise more than one corpse at a time and can raise deadly armies. However, a corpse can only be raised by one necromancer, and once that corpse is released from a necromancer's control, only that necromancer can bring them back."

—Braekios Journal #10, page 31

One night, something woke me, but a glance around my room showed no threat. My heart raced and it wasn't until I coughed that I realized there was smoke in the air. It was the middle of the dry season, and the townspeople knew better than to burn anything besides a body, so I rushed to get dressed, knowing that my help would be needed and appreciated.

I ran into town but stopped abruptly at the edge of the main square. The screams, moans, and crunching formed a cacophony that held my body hostage as I took in the sight in front of me. Buildings burned and a large motley group of corpses meandered among a group of dead townspeople, occasionally picking up an arm to sniff at it, or kicking at a face to see if the person was truly dead. I noticed that a few of the corpses were bleeding or had knives and other random weapons still stuck fast in their body. But the living feel pain while the dead don't, so nothing stopped the corpses from killing their attackers.

"Oh, there it is! That smell! I'd know it anywhere! Nectar. It's been so long, give it to me!" The words reached me at the same time he did.

Looking at the necromancer in front of me, I knew I would've turned out like him if Imogene hadn't taken me in. His skin was pulled tight, with bones eager to escape their shell. The shredded shirt he wore did nothing to hide the bloated stomach that only starvation could give. His black hair was matted and fell in long, dirty waves over his face, preventing me from seeing anything beyond his black pupils.

He moved closer to me and sniffed. "It's coming from you!! Do you have it? You must give it to me, you must, you must!" His words were punctuated with lunges towards my arms.

One of his long, ragged fingernails grazed my arm and drew blood. He stared at it before taking my arm in his grimy hands and raising it to his mouth. I shuddered as he took a long languid lick across the cut. His head tilted back towards the moon and an ecstatic smile grew. I tried to pull out of his grip, but his hands tightened into a crushing hold.

"It's in your blood, what incredibly good luck I have! You taste delicious and now I won't have to beg him for more. I've wandered for so long, occasionally catching a scent here and there. Oh yes, you made it difficult, but it will be all worth it."

He continued to speak about hiding me somewhere only he knew, but my brain was stuck on his words. What was Nectar? I gave my shirt a quick sniff but didn't smell anything off. As curious as I was, the threat of death loomed, and I forced the panic down in order to think calmly. Men, human or other, react to getting kicked in the balls the same way. I brought my foot between his legs forcibly and as he bent over, I turned to run, hoping to lock myself back home and wait for this nightmare to be over, only for two corpses to block my way and hold me in place.

"That was not very nice." he said, slowly rising from the crouch I put him into. He winced slightly before continuing, "You should feel honored to serve a purpose. I think I'll suspend you and lie underneath, so I can watch your sweet, sweet blood drip into my mouth." He caressed my throat with calloused fingertips before turning back to the road. He sighed and stepped towards the woods that the road disappeared into, a gesture to the corpses holding me had them dragging me after him, my struggle not slowing them an inch.

"No, please! Let me go!" I cried, dropping to my knees, hoping that my sudden change would make them pause for a second, just to be dragged on my knees instead of my feet. "I can help you. I know what the song sounds like, and I know how to make it stop! Please!"

Surprisingly, he did stop, and I felt my heart skip a beat with the sudden swell of hope I felt. "I have no idea what the song is, but why would I want my gifts hindered?" My hope fell away like a tree shedding its leaves, only to be replaced by the certainty of my death. "Because of it, I'm never lonely." At this, some of the corpses who still ravaged the town gathered around him and he petted their heads like obedient little dogs. "Now, no more. I tire of this simple place."

We walked again and while my body hung limp, my mind strove to find something, anything, and it was then that I became aware of the tincture I took yesterday wearing off.

In the darkness of my mind was a chorus, growing louder with each second. I embraced it, quickly adding my voice to the melody. Humming, feeling the glory of the symphony saturated my bones and skin in a song too rich to stay in my head. I was the conductor, and I raised their voices into a crescendo, feeling their bodies rise to wakefulness at the same time. Our minds now one, I saw what happened before I arrived. The buildings were fed to the flames held by the corpses who laid in wait for the inhabitants to run out before catching them and dragging them into the middle of the courtyard. Each person was held as the necromancer sniffed at their face. With a shake of the necromancer's head their fates were decided, and they were killed quickly. With each new death, the townspeople grew angrier, and some decided to fight back, only to be struck down. The only relief I felt was that they were killed with more mercy than I thought the necromancer was capable of.

I laughed, a sound so cynical and manic, and I watched fear enter the necromancer's eyes. I knew what he saw. Knew that all the people he slaughtered rose to their feet, all ready to follow my commands. With a flick of my head, they turned on their captors, working together to tear limbs off, crack open heads, and put down anything that held them. The butcher used his knife to hack down two corpses before feeding them into a fire. A group of children used strings from their pajamas to climb up bodies twice their size, garroting them before jumping back down. When the necromancer saw that he'd lost control of this battle he ran off, quickly disappearing down the road, the two corpses holding me trailing after him.

As he disappeared over the horizon, the bodies not re-killed by my town fell to the ground, useless without their master in range. Exela was a moving necropolis, but it was still home to these deceased people and its one living resident. I knew that we could go on and keep this night secret. After all, they were part of me now, and I could keep a secret.

I walked among them, taking note of the damaged well and the buildings still smoldering from fires set during the night.

"What to do now?" I thought as the recently killed and now re-animated townspeople gathered around me. "This is our home. You've destroyed it. You'll rebuild it, and we'll go back to our lives."

I gave out orders to burn the enemy bodies and rebuild before returning home, knowing that a certain cat waited for me. As Trickster rubbed against me, purring with all his dead little heart could manage, I took note of the progress made during the night. And day. The best part of having a dead workforce was that they didn't need sleep or other breaks, and by the next week, the town returned to its peaceful self. I increased the illusion, trying to make everything normal again by creating conversations around me, adding laughter and smiles.

The attack taught me one thing, that there was clearly more I could do with my powers and my knowledge. I could find the necromancers like me, the ones who wanted a normal life, and give them Philipa's Tincture. I refused to accept that I was the only one who didn't want to be a monster. I spent the next month in my workroom, determined to make a tincture that could withstand larger groups for longer.

I had a new version ready to be tested, when something odd echoed through the song I held in my mind. They shared a song about a visitor, the first we had received since the attack, and I had them do nothing until I could observe this person. Walking through Exela, I silently looked for a tall woman with an athletic build, wearing tight brown pants and an olive-green shirt that had signs of being worn frequently. According to the townspeople, her hair was brown and cropped to her ears, or rather her ear, since she was missing one.

I turned the next corner and saw her crouch in front of a young boy as she played with a dagger in her hand. I couldn't make out most of what she said, but I did catch the words "the Order" and knew I was being presented with an opportunity. Imogene had told me of them and their purpose, warning me to never let them know of my powers. I needed to quickly and quietly convince this woman that I was not a threat. Perhaps I could convince her of my usefulness and sway her to my cause. Approaching her from behind, I had the townspeople draw near to cover my actions and make me invisible. As she turned around and faced them, her hands out in front of her and saying, "I'm here to help," I slipped around her and used a stone I'd worked free from the road to swiftly hit her on the back of her head. I caught her as she fell and had two of the townspeople bring her back into my house. She was promptly tied to the table, and I pulled up a chair next to her. I waited, trying to find the words I would use and hoping that I didn't hit her across the head too hard.

Chapter Eight — Lysandra

"Once a necromancer manifests their abilities, there is nothing that can be done to return them to their human state. There is no cure for necromancy, only a lethal blow can end the existence that causes so much pain and suffering."

—Braekios Journal #5, page 5

Have you ever gotten too close to a nest of angry bees? My head felt like that, full of buzzing and sharp stings pricking the inside of my brain at random. My eyes stayed shut as I tried to assess my surroundings. Rotating my wrists led me to feel the ropes that kept me restrained to what I assumed was a floor, but after a quick jiggle of my legs determined it was a table.

"I know you're awake," came a light, quiet voice.

Not feeling the need to pretend to be okay, I let out the groan I was holding in and picked my head up, trying to see where the voice came from and take in everything that this room was. Sunlight came in through four open windows in front of me, and the rays hit the crystals strung across the ceiling. The stones reflected the sunlight onto the walls, turning them into sharply pointed rainbows that moved with the wind that came in. Plants took up all the livable space in the room, crammed into every corner. Some hung upside-down from the ceiling, drying, while others were potted and reaching towards the ceiling. Through the wall-mounted jungle, the sun reflected off the glass jars showing the odd liquids and clumps held inside.

My eyes slid to the woman plucking leaves off a dead plant, humming along to a song I couldn't hear. Her long blond hair was pulled back into a practical bun, and she wore loose tan pants stained with different shades of brown and green. The once white, now gray shirt tucked into the pants were rolled up to her elbows, where random pastes, glues and dirt were smeared.

When she turned around, I saw that the smears extended up to her face around her odd black glasses.

Before I could decide that speaking was maybe not a good idea, my traitorous mouth opened and said, "I have to ask, what's with the glasses? Are you blind? Or have some kind of deformity?"

She touched them self-consciously before pulling a chair over and answered, "I'm neither blind nor deformed. I happen to have an extreme light sensitivity, and these help me." She placed her head in her hands that rested on the table near where my hands stayed balled up, and I assumed she stared at me through the glasses. "This is a small town, the only visitors we get are traveling merchants. Why don't you tell me who you are and why you're here?"

I tried to state my purpose again, hoping that I would be successful this time unlike the conversations I had. "I work for an organization who protects people from necromancy. I was told that the people here were in danger, so I came to investigate."

"There could be a necromancer here? Wouldn't I know?" There was something in her tone that I didn't quite like, but I couldn't figure out why.

"Normally, yes, you would, but this one seems to be much more subtle than most. Have you noticed anything weird? Anyone not acting like themself, or a sudden lack of animals? It could be that they're still here and hiding."

She brought a finger to her lips as she considered the question. "Well," she said with a sing-song lilt, "we've gotten more rain than normal, but I don't think that's what you mean."

That was a bullshit answer if I ever did hear one.

"Look," I mumbled, yanking at the ropes on my wrists. "Let me go so I can get back to my job. If I don't see anything weird, I'll be on my way. I haven't hurt anyone, and I have no intention of hurting you, so can you untie me?"

"Oh, I think you do have the intention of hurting me."

I was starting to get pissed off. Who the fuck was this woman?

"Unless you're the necromancer I'm here to kill, which I don't think you are because you don't seem batshit crazy, I'm not going to so much as pluck out one of those pretty blonde hairs!"

"How can you be certain that there's a necromancer here?" Her head tilted.

"A merchant came to us with a story of being refused entry to this town by people who seemed not to recognize him, despite being close friends. They looked ill and didn't seem to be breathing, so he was worried that there was something strange going on here. That crowd out there was not among the living, so I have to go hunt down the necromancer since you're clearly not it."

"But I am." The chill in her voice and the way she walked her fingers up my stomach raised alarm bells.

"Am what?" I asked, hoping that I didn't screw up so spectacularly as to be held hostage by my enemy.

"I'm the necromancer," she confirmed, and all I could do was stare at her, needing it to be a joke.

"Boop," she said, lightly touching my nose. My brain froze on the bizarre act, and I scrambled to regain control of this situation.

"Prove it." Proof, I needed proof that she wasn't human. After removing her glasses, she brought her face inches away from mine and I stared up into eyes as silver as starshine. I felt fear turn my blood to ice. I was unarmed and incapacitated, the two things that meant an upcoming, gruesome death. I tugged harder at my bonds, determined to break free, as it laughed and kissed my nose before backing up to lean against the wall.

"I don't know what type of torture this is but let me go and I'll grant you a merciful death." It's laugh made me pause. Those silver eyes held the mania I associated with necromancers, but they were also sad, and pleading, things I wasn't aware monsters felt. It sat back in its chair again, bringing us eye to eye but out of biting range. I wasn't thrilled with the idea of having necromantic blood in my mouth, but if biting off its nose or ear bought me enough time to escape, then so be it.

"Aren't you going to say something like, let me go and I'll forget about you? I must admit, I'm not feeling enticed to untie you. I rather like living." It prattled while using a finger to stroke my nose again. Up and down the finger went, brushing over me like she lulled a pet to sleep.

A ragged-looking cat came in and brushed against its legs. A fond smile crossed the necromancer's face, and it bent down to pet it. The cat let out a crackling meow and licked the hand that petted it.

"What's that?" The cat looked ancient and on the verge of death, and I wondered who'd die first, the cat or the Preceptor of the Order.

"This," it said, lifting the creature up so I could see it, "is Trickster."

The cat was placed on me, where it kneaded my stomach with sharp claws.

"Okay, sure. Since when do necromancers have pets?" I asked between dodging the paws as the cat now decided my nose looked like a new toy.

"Since the lonely young necromancer and the kitten that no one wanted were introduced," it responded, watching the cat do its best to give me some new facial scars.

"Right." Sure, why couldn't a scary, murderous necromancer have a familiar? Returning to the more important matter, I tried a different tactic. "Look, let me go and I'll give you directions to a mass grave I passed on the way here. It's full of bodies itching for an afterlife."

It was a lie, I had no idea where to find recent kills, but it didn't need to know that. Hoping that would finally convince this odd monster to let me go, I was disheartened when her nose wrinkled in distaste.

"That's simply repulsive, and I can't believe you offered that," it said scornfully.

I groaned again and growled, "I can think of anything else to offer you, so why don't you tell me what you want!"

It seemed to be wrestling with a thought, but after a few seconds of silence punctuated by the occasional *mlem* of the cat cleaning itself, all the while on my stomach, it spoke.

"I want you to hear me out, and I want to help." The necromancer's voice was quieter and more unsure than I'd heard it so far.

"Help with what?" There was no way I couldn't be suspicious.

"I'll get to that. First, you should know that while I haven't always been blessed with these gifts—" My eyebrows shot up at the words blessed and gifts "—I've always studied botany and medicine. I happen to serve as the apothecary for Exela and what I've learned, I learned from one of the smartest people I knew. I'm going to tell you a story, but before I do, I'm going to make you a little more comfortable."

My mind strategized but came to a halt with the next sentence. "If you attempt to escape, or cause any harm to myself or Trickster, I'll have one of the many corpses stationed outside this room kill you with your own weapons. Which would you prefer to receive the killing blow from? The hatchet? The dagger? Or perhaps I'll have them use the brass knuckles to bash your head open."

I reluctantly let it transfer me to a chair, my wrists and ankles already chafing from the constant bindings. I was offered the cup of water that originally rested on a little side table near the door, but I refused despite my parched mouth; I had no idea what this necromancer, formerly an apothecary, may have put in it. It rolled its eyes before taking a sip and showing an elaborate display of swallowing the water. I waited for an agonizingly long minute, ensuring it was not a toxin with a delayed reaction, before allowing it to give me some water. I drained that cup and the next, hoping that it didn't contain a poison safe for necromancers but lethal to humans. It was silent for a few minutes as the necromancer sat back down and settled the wretched cat on its lap. The cat took one last wary look at me before tucking its tail against its body and going to sleep.

"Once upon a time, there was a girl and her mother who traveled with the wind."

The sun set on the weirdest day of my life and my stomach rumbled, pulling both of us back into the present.

"Look, we all have tragic backstories. You never knew your father, which sounds like a good thing, and your mother told you to kill yourself. Mine sold me when they didn't want to be parents anymore. Spare me the sob story. None of this means anything to me, but if you bring me some food, I'd be willing to wait long enough for you to tell me the point of all this before I find some incredibly creative way to escape and kill you."

It huffed but left to put dinner together. The smell of something cooking was the sign I waited for, and I rocked the chair. Slowly, I gathered enough momentum to knock myself into the shelf of glass jars behind me. Shards of glass and odd colored liquids fell on me as I struggled to catch my breath, winded from the fall. The sound of breaking glass and wood no doubt could be heard from the kitchen and the clock ticking near the door reminded me of the precious few seconds I had before being discovered. My fingers moved frantically through the glass shards, looking for a big enough piece before I finally found a large, rounded piece with a sharp point. My palm bled from the tiny pieces I skipped over, but I managed to saw through one of the bonds and quickly freed my other hand and feet.

I found my weapons and travel pack stacked neatly in a corner and managed to take a step into the hall before the necromancer came running around the corner, eyes frantically darting around. When they landed on me, its eyebrows furrowed. I figured out what it had done when I heard loud banging coming from behind the main door. Reinforcements were called in and I was out of time.

I did the only thing I could think of and rushed at it, dagger in my left hand only briefly before I pressed it against the monster's neck. My hand tangled in its blond hair, and I walked us into the hall, pushing it against the stone-cold wall. Outside, the pounding stopped, no doubt the corpses awaited further orders.

I used the few inches I had over it in height to leer down at it, my body still and tense. "Tell me why I shouldn't kill you right now." Fury settled within me, and I tried not to let it affect my decision making, determined to at least try to hear out the necromancer.

"I can help. I want to help," it whispered, trying and failing to inch the dagger away from its throat with a shaking hand. "I can craft a tincture that nullifies necromantic abilities. It will instantly render the reanimated deceased and dull the madness, for a little while."

"Why should I believe you?"

This wasn't possible, if it were true, Braekios would've known about it, right? As the necromancer let out a shaky breath the dagger lightly pricked its throat and I watched as a drop of blood welled up, as red as a human's.

It gestured towards the room behind us. "I have a vial in my workroom. I made it recently but haven't had the chance to test its potency. Let's bring some of the dead inside, I'll drink it, and you can see that I'm telling the truth."

"Sure, that sounds like a great idea. I'll let you bring in some of your dead buddies and they'll swarm me and make me join your legion of doom. How will I know you didn't release them and pretend to have lost your powers?"

It peered up into my eyes. "It's not as if I want to raise them, you know. I can't resist the song, even if I wanted to. You've fought enough necromancers, I'm pretty sure you know what madness and humanity looks like. Even if you didn't know the difference, I'm not an actress, there's no way I'd be able to fool you."

I smiled, letting the necromancer see my canines. "You're right, I've fought necromancers. I know how to kill them, mercilessly, and more importantly, I know not to trust them. Why would I even consider letting you go long enough to get this tincture?"

"What have you got to lose?" It asked, exasperatedly.

"My life for one," I responded, equally exasperated.

"Sure, you could die. But if you don't, you'll bring your Order a powerful new tool."

Those were the exact right words to say. It was the only way to make me agree to this plan. I've lived my life for the Order, for the cause. I could sacrifice my potential future if it meant giving others the chance of having one.

"Fine," I spat, hating the way the agreement tasted in my mouth. "How long will this experiment last? Because I have places that aren't here to visit."

"I don't want to do this either. The last thing I want to do is be shadowed by someone who's actively plotting my death. Past versions of Philipa's Tincture have lasted up to three weeks, but the most recent one didn't last more than a day against all the deceased townspeople. I'm hoping that this new version can withstand larger presences for longer. A week, if my calculations are correct."

"You want me to watch you, surrounded by multiple rotting corpses, for a week?!" No way, there was no fucking way I was doing this.

"You won't be the only one here. Trust me, I'm not thrilled to be trapped in here for a week either."

Good to know that we'd both be miserable.

"If we do this, we're setting some rules. You will not spend any time outside of my vision, except using the bathroom. But I'll be outside the door, and you will do your business with that door cracked. If you're not using the bathroom, you will be tied up, and yes, that does include when sleeping. If you make any move towards me, or if I hear a dead buddy of yours inching closer, I'll kill you and I'll make it slow and painful. I've been doing this for a very long time, so trust that I know how to bleed you out slowly. Do we have an agreement?"

It didn't even hesitate, which surprised me slightly. If anything, it looked relieved, as if this was the best outcome it could wish for, despite the threat of death.

"Yes! Yes, I agree. I promise that if I put so much as a toe out of your determined line, I'll welcome my murder."

It bounced on its feet, much as a child would when it was about to receive a piece of candy or a new toy, before stopping when the knife dug in a little bit closer to its throat. Did this thing not have any sort of self-preservation?

It stuck out its hand, and the eyes that held mine didn't blink as it waited for me to seal the deal. Would I be turning my back on the Order by working with the thing we were created to kill? If Dinah were here, would she have sliced the throat in front of her before a word came out of its mouth? Ultimately, it didn't matter, I was the only one here and it was my decision. I took the offered hand and shook it gently, feeling calluses across its palm that felt so like my own.

There was something darkly satisfying about using the remaining ropes that were on me to tie the necromancer together, and while I made sure they'd be loose enough to not chafe easily, the hands and feet were tied close enough together to prevent the necromancer from choking me or being able to do anything more than shuffle around.

We agreed to use one of the empty bedrooms as a crypt and we watched as the dead paraded in, forming orderly lines as they entered the dark room. I kept my back against the wall and the necromancer in front of me. If one of the corpses decided to attack me it would need to reach beyond the necromancer, and that could buy me the few seconds I needed to launch a counterattack and escape.

Only once we closed and locked the door did I remove the dagger from its throat. I followed it back into the workroom, and watched as it rummaged around the shelves, before pulling out a small round vial with a muddy-looking liquid.

"Here goes everything," it said and drank the nasty smelling liquid, its eyes closed tight, and nose wrinkled as if to repel what I must assume tasted as good as decay smells.

I had to take a step back when its eyes opened at last. It was as if a film was removed from them and while I'd thought the eyes bright before, I now found them luminous. Yet the brightness didn't outshine the smile that stretched from ear to ear, and I noticed the slight crow's feet near the corner of the necromancer's eyes. For some reason this made me uncomfortable, and it took me a few seconds to realize it was due to the necromancer having a feature I only associated only with humans.

"It's quiet again. I can't hear anyone except myself," was all it said before walking over and gingerly picking up the cat who'd fallen over from where it walked. I hadn't noticed that it stopped moving, yet another sign that this whole situation was wildly outside of my comfort zone.

The tenderness it held the cat with while placing it on a pile of blankets in the bedroom had my brain scrambling to fit into the image of a typical necromancer I had in my head. I stopped that line of thinking before my brain dangerously categorized it as something else. It followed me to the crypt, and I heard it take a deep breath in as I unlocked the door to see piles of corpses lying around, unmoving once again.

"I need to write this down," the necromancer mumbled after releasing the breath it held, searching for a leather-bound notebook and a pen.

Yet again we walked back to the work room, and I had the feeling that I would be spending a lot of time in the small room. It settled back down at the worktable, and I saw that it was annoyed at the binds, glancing at me whenever the ropes made it awkward to write.

I smiled back and waved with Dinah's dagger, both an invitation and a threat.

After a while it spoke up, its voice a little anxious. "Now that we're going to be around each other a lot, what should I call you?"

It didn't even cross my mind to give a false name. "I'm Lysandra but call me Lys."

"Talia."

Chapter Nine — Talia

"Necromancers are the apex predator, and until now there have been no challenges to their rule. We will learn to track, fight, and kill, serving as a shield for those who can't fight for themselves. We will turn away no one, offering a home and income for those who choose to join us."

—Braekios Journal #10, page 43

Every move I made had me questioning if it was going to be my last. Did I cut the vegetables for dinner a little too briskly and Lys thought I imagined her death? When I stumbled after her down the hall after trying to take a bigger step than I could, did she think it was to throw her down and choke her? Since we were stuck in the house until the tincture wore off, there was nothing to do except worry, pace, and refill my stock of medicinals with my dried plants. When the restock was done, there was nothing to do except keep my mind constantly searching the darkness for a voice or a hint of the song. By the third day, my nail beds were destroyed from the constant picking, my legs were sore from the constant walking, and I was pretty sure Lys was going to kill me out of sheer annoyance.

Lys, meanwhile, found a routine quickly. Upon waking up in the morning, she'd do stretches in our bedroom before running through hand-to-hand combat dances until sweat dripped. After several repetitions of the dances, I'd help her push the furniture to the edges, and she'd begin weapon dances that held my gaze. The way her hatchet and daggers whirled through the air was hypnotizing and as the sunlight reflected off the metal occasionally, I was practically lulled to sleep. Somehow, she still had the energy to do more and took to the halls to run laps up and down. Finally done with all her self-inflicted torture, she'd lead me into the bathroom where she'd scrub herself clean and I'd stand in the corner facing away from the very naked woman in the tub. It was well into the day when we'd finally eat our first meal. She'd spend the afternoons perusing the books I'd stacked throughout the house and watching me do the little work I had to keep me occupied. The sun would set, and we'd travel into the kitchen where she'd handle slicing the vegetables and meat. I tried to prepare the food the first night, but the second my hand touched the knife she plucked it from me and shot me a withering look. The tension kept us frozen for a few beats until she realized I wasn't making a move against her. With a gesture, she sent me to wash the vegetables and began to expertly slice the chicken. When it seemed like she was perfectly content to stay in this locked house, doing the same thing every day, I looked closer. In the few minutes we were sitting down, or she wasn't exercising, her foot tapped, or her finger drew imaginary swirls into the table and chair arms.

When she glared at me while sharpening her dagger, I decided to read one of my favorite books, but my mind couldn't help but return to the mystery of the woman who was now doing an absurd number of push-ups in front of me, for the second time that day, deviating from her usual routine. Our prison seemed to be shrinking in on her, maybe this was finally the time to ask some questions of my own.

"You mentioned coming here for your job. What is it that you do, exactly?" I asked softly, my eyes unable to look away from the muscles rippling in her shoulders as she went up and down.

I needed this conversation to be interesting enough to hold my attention for a couple of minutes, or if I was very lucky, a couple of hours. Since deciding I wasn't a threat without my powers, she'd changed out of her fighting leathers as well as the personal armory she attached to her when not engaging in some sort of masochistic exercise regime that was a form of torture. During the day she wore a loose long sleeve cotton shirt and light brown pants that had pockets I envied, but right now I got a great view of the scars that seemed to cover every inch of her body, thanks to the pants and very simple and very thin breast band she currently wore.

"I'm a chasseur of the Order of Braekios," she grunted in-between push-ups. I knew of the Order, but not who it was named after.

"I've heard of the name, but I don't know anything about them besides the fact that they kill necromancers."

She stopped and rose into a sitting position and whisked the sweat away from her skin. "That's all?"

When I shrugged, she looked bewildered. "But you're a necromancer. No one told you about the man who first started looking for monsters like you?"

"Wow, thanks for the reminder," I muttered, but she didn't hear me and continued.

"When the demonic offspring of Fae and humans grew up, they felt they were superior and wanted to pick up where their Fae parents left off, with killing the humans. The first generation of necromancers were way more powerful than modern day ones, all thanks to the amount of Fae blood they had, so you can imagine the havoc they caused. A lot of people died. When I say a lot, I mean the human species almost went extinct between the war with the Fae and now these random attacks from necromancers. Then one day a sadistic bastard named Braekios decided to, um, learn the ins and outs of necromancers and record all his findings. The Order was formed using his notes to hunt and kill necromancers."

"Why did you join them? Aren't there less dangerous, equally adventurous professions out there?"

She looked at me as if I was simple-minded. "I didn't join willingly. Do you remember how I said my parents sold me? It was the Order they received their payment from. I may call myself a chasseur and say that I have free will, but I'm an indentured servant, who will serve the Order until I die."

I didn't know what to say, and an awkward silence began to fester until I blurted out, "When my mother left, all I had was a letter from her. She didn't say goodbye in it, only that I was better off dead and that if I valued humanity, I'd kill myself. I know what it's like, feeling like you have a life sentence you can't escape."

That got her attention. "That was cruel and unfair of her. You didn't choose to be a necromancer, it's genetic, unfortunately." Her surprising kindness put a lump in my throat that I was unable to speak around.

She seemed to sense that I couldn't speak because she said something about it being time to eat and pushed me to the kitchen.

That night I couldn't sleep. I tossed around in bed trying to get comfortable around the bindings, grateful that I wasn't tied to the bed. Was my mother cruel? I hadn't considered it but looking at my childhood, I saw my mother being aloof instead of caring, distant instead of involved, and self-preserving instead of vulnerable. Maybe that was cruelty, but unseen because of the rose-colored glasses that was youth. My foot itched, and I bent down only to stop short when my bound hands didn't allow the movement. By bringing my foot up instead of reaching down, I was able to use the roughness of the cord binding my hands together to soothe the itch.

At least I was able to roll over instead of staring at the ceiling all night. It was the only slightly comfortable thing about my new sleeping arrangements, and yet it was still above the experience of sleeping next to a person who actively wanted to kill me.

A low, pained moan reached my ears and I turned to see Lys thrashing from side to side, her limbs extending at weird angles before jerking into a different, uncomfortable position.

When her moan turned into a scream, I scooted off the bed and hobbled over to her. My hopes to gently shake her from her nightmare were thrown out the second my hands touched her shoulder. Her eyes sprung open, and I found myself on my back, her forearm pressing into my windpipe as she leveraged her strength against me. Wild and angry eyes locked with mine and I could tell that she wasn't seeing me as she slowly pressed down harder on my throat. My legs flailed uselessly behind us as I tried to push her off me, but my hands felt heavy as it became hard to breath.

I managed to gasp out, "Lys please!" before the blackness of the night claimed me.

I was surprised when I woke up the next morning, so sure that last night was going to be my last. My mouth was dry, and when pain shot through me as I tried to clear my throat, I recalled the way my windpipe was slowly forced in on itself. I resisted gulping down a breath of air as I looked for Lys.

"I wouldn't try speaking yet. I managed to stop before I killed you, but I got close. You'll probably have trouble swallowing for a few days." Lys sat on the edge of the bed staring at me, and I blinked.

The image of her hunched over and hugging her knees made her look like a child expecting to be reprimanded. It was so at odds with the sarcastic, tough person I grew to know over these past few days that I inhaled sharply before letting out hacking coughs.

In the silence that followed she said, "I'm so sorry, I was stuck reliving my worst day. When I opened my eyes to see yours, I was back there, fighting and losing, and my body fell back on instincts I gained the hard way. I would've killed you if you hadn't whispered my name.

No matter what I'm doing, I need you to stay away from me when I sleep. I can't risk losing your tincture because you tried to wake me up and I killed you in my sleep."

I nodded and she helped me off the bed. It was only then that I realized my hands were untied.

Her cheeks turned pink as she tried to explain. "Since I'm the only one who knows where the keys to the house are hidden and you apparently don't know how to fight back, I figured I'd let you sleep untied. One of us should be able to get a good night's rest. "

She looked away briefly, embarrassed, before finishing. "But," and her eyes turned cold again, "if you threaten me or try to find the keys to let in your puppets, I won't hesitate again. You'll be dead before you can even try to reanimate something."

With one last vicious smile she walked out of the room, leaving me feeling unsettled. I thought we'd moved past the whole monster business. She knew I was half human, why was that the half that was harder to see? Didn't I bleed red like her? The only thing that gave away my Fae heritage were my eyes, so why couldn't she see my human hands, or hear the way my heart beat the same way hers did? The slight sting in my throat reminded me of what she was capable and willing to do if I couldn't follow her instructions to the letter.

Breakfast was quiet, quieter than it's been, and the mistrust between us seemed to make the air thick with suspicion. I was going to scream, I needed to get out of this house or else my anxiety was going to be the cause of my death instead of Lys. I saw her hand reach for the dagger at the clang my spoon made hitting the bowl and I reached my limit.

"That's it," I said, rising to my feet, Lys eying me warily. "If you're going to kill me, it's going to be in the fresh air and not in this crypt."

Now she rose, too. "Oh, really? How do I know you're not going to run off the second we leave the house?"

I opened my mouth to shout at her but stopped when I saw the way her eyes turned from suspicious to eager. She was as desperate to get out of the house as I was.

"Please, where would I go? You traveled here from Braeton, you know how far the nearest town is, and the next traveling merchant isn't due for a couple of weeks, so I couldn't even catch a ride if I wanted to. There's a lake not far from here that has some herbs and plants that I need. Let's go down and while I gather what I need, you can go for a jog, or a swim. "

I saw that she considered the idea, and I tried one last attempt. "I've seen you looking out the windows. You can't deny that you're tired of running laps around these halls. We won't be gone for long, just long enough for us to soak in the sun and get some vitamin D."

She gave a sharp nod and we quickly packed up some empty jars, thick work gloves, pruning scissors and jugs of water. The door was shoved open, its hinges squeaking loudly from days without use, and as the sun reached our faces, we took deep, greedy breaths of the crisp morning air.

"We're only going for a few hours. To stretch our legs," Lys said as we stepped out onto the road.

We spent the entire day there. The sun kissed our skin and as a gentle breeze rustled my hair, I plucked and prepared plants while Lys ran lap after lap around the lake. Each glance I got of her face as she ran by was borderline ecstatic. She still ran by the time I'd plucked, pruned, and bottled everything, so I sat down and stretched my legs out, determined to make the sensation of the sun last as long as possible. I had no idea how she could run for so long, let alone how she could enjoy it, but the wink and grin she sent my way on her last lap made it clear that she was having a great time. Seeing her laugh and relax had me releasing the tension that had been calling my body home for these past couple of days. I was still terrified of her, and yet in this moment she reminded me of a dog, happy to be let loose from her leash.

She came over to me, said something about washing off, undressed before I was able to turn around, making me blush from my ears to my toes as I stared at anything besides her newly naked form. She ran into the lake, and I buried my head in my hands for a second, forcing my body to calm down. I heard a splash and looked up to see bubbles on the surface indicating where Lys had submerged. I tried to guess where she'd be coming up for air, but as the seconds got longer, I grew worried. My shirt was off, and my pants were around my ankles by the time she finally reemerged, a gasp coming from both her and me. I fell back onto my butt as I tried to redress and she stood there the entire time watching me, grinning as she dripped water.

"I caught lunch!" She said as my eyes flew to the wriggling fish in her hand. Plenty of kids tried to catch fish with their hands while we grew up, but none succeeded. Was there anything this strange woman couldn't do?

She gutted and scaled the fish as I prepared a fire, grateful, for this one moment, that we hadn't had any rain in a while. We ate in companionable silence, but I felt her desire to ask a question.

I swallowed the last bite and decided she'd squirmed enough, so I asked. "What is it? You clearly have something on your mind, ask."

She didn't have the dignity to look sheepish, choosing only to scoot closer to me before asking, "You said you can't resist the song. What is it?"

I've never had to explain it to anyone, even Imogene accepted it as a mystery, so I had to formulate an answer before responding.

"It's what I call the pull of necromantic power I feel around dead things. I have no idea if it's the same for all necromancers, but when I'm around a body, I hear its voice in my mind. I call it the song because the voice rises and falls in pitches and each body has its own rhythm. I think what I hear is the soul of that person, reaching out to me, and only once I respond with my own do we become one and the body rises."

I had barely finished my response when she asked her next question. "How do they communicate with you? Are they intelligent enough to form sentences?"

"Huh, I never thought about what I hear." I paused, thinking through all the times I heard the song. "No, they don't use words, I usually hear a hum or vocalization. They can communicate, though, through images and feelings. It's how I found you that first day. Your presence sent a ripple through my mind, and I pieced together where to find you based on what the townspeople saw."

Lys had been writing in a small notebook she produced from her bag. She saw me watching and pink slowly grew across her cheeks and ear.

She squirmed and tried to provide an explanation. "This is the first time besides Braekios that someone's been able to get answers from a necromancer without having to, you know…"

"Torture them?" I supplied when it was clear she didn't want to finish the sentence.

She cleared her throat, and it surprised me to see that she seemed ashamed of what the Order did to the necromancers it didn't kill right away.

"Can I ask you something?" I hoped she didn't find this the reason to kill me.

"Sure," was her response as she sprawled out on the grass, her head crushing little yellow flowers under it.

"You ate the fish, but whenever we eat a meal with some kind of meat, you put it on my plate. What's that all about?"

She sighed and rubbed her eyes. "I was chasing after a necromancer that slaughtered a neighboring town. It was early fall, warm, and by the time we got there the bodies had been rotting for a while. The smell was, well, you can imagine." I could and shuddered. "Since then, I haven't been able to eat meat. It always brings me back to that day."

I didn't know what else to say, but I wasn't ready to return to the house, so I needed to keep her talking. Thankfully there was still something that we needed to discuss. "It's been almost five days, and I expect the tincture to wear off soon. We need to have a plan for when that happens. "

I braced myself for her response, expecting an outburst, or for her to unsheathe her hatchet. Instead, she turned to a new page to take notes and I hoped that she didn't intend to share them with the Order. I wasn't sure that I was ready for them to know me that intimately.

"The biggest threat, as you know, will be the corpses. While we did lock a significant amount away in the bedroom and you locked the front door, with enough force they could break in. I wish I could tell you with certainty that I wouldn't immediately call them to me, but I have no idea what the madness will require me to do. Prepare to fight corpses, but you won't need to kill them all. This is the updated version of Philipa's Tincture that I last drank." I handed over one of the spares I had and watched her gently put it into her pack. "Force that down my throat and it'll hopefully take effect immediately, causing the corpses to fall. Hopefully it won't come to a fight. I've grown used to the sensation of the madness creeping back and I anticipate feeling it wearing off. When I first feel the madness again, I'll take the tincture, hopefully before I raise

any corpses. But given the number of corpses around us, I have a feeling I'll be quickly

overwhelmed and taken by the madness. If I drink the tincture and the corpses still move, you

have to kill me. I have spares of the tincture in the work room, you can take one to your Order

and have them analyze it."

Her eyes narrowed, and her body stilled the way only a predator's does before attacking.

"Why shouldn't I kill you now that I know where the tincture is?" She asked, and I forced myself

to move past the sting of betrayal that ran through my body.

"Because," I said, glad that I took the proper precautions to ensure my life, "I may have

left the tincture available, but I've hidden my notes regarding its preparation. It took years for

Imogene and me to create it, I can't imagine it would be easy for the Order to figure out the

intricate process it took to make. You need me alive, remember? You need my knowledge."

"I know," was all she said, and her body relaxed once more as she finished writing her

notes.

She pocketed the notebook, and I shifted where I sat, still uneasy from how quick she was

to decide to kill me only to back away from the idea. I may have Fae blood in me, but her

capriciousness had me questioning, if maybe, just maybe, she had a drop of Fae blood in her too.

Her eyes moved around, looking for something else to talk about until they settled on the

discarded petals, and stems nearby.

"What do you do with all of this? I know you used it to make the tincture, but I don't

understand how. I have a basic understanding of medicine, and I make a balm to help my

wounds heal, but that's about it. This tincture you made puts all of that to shame. Are you sure it's not an extension of your powers?" Her curious eyes turned suspicious, and I answered quickly before she distrusted me even more.

"My tincture's like most medicines; it has a unique blend of ingredients prepared. But you'd be amazed at what can be made with what can be found here." I stood up and pulled her to her feet. "Let me show you," I said, gesturing to the little yellow flowers nearby.

The rest of the afternoon was spent teaching her the knowledge that Imogene passed down to me. Watching Lys interact with plants with a softness she hadn't shown me made my heart constrict in my chest. It was impossible not to think of Imogene and the child I once was. Imogene would've handled Lys and this whole situation so much better. She would've sat Lys down, forced her to see reason, and would've tutted that Lys looked in desperate need of a warm drink. Soon, they would've been drinking tea and laughing about the miscommunication. I missed her so much, it felt like my heart would never be whole again. I had no idea what I was doing, let alone how I was going to convince the rest of the Order that I was more valuable alive as an herbalist rather than a threat handled with historical and lethal prejudice.

The sun started to set, the oranges and reds making the lake look like it was made of fire, and we trudged up the path to town and back to the house. The tightness in my chest returned with every step and I already missed our time at the lake. Judging by the way Lys massaged the shoulders that had crept back up to her ear, I could tell that she felt the same way. We passed by the little house I once called home and I paused. When we first trekked down to the lake, I refused to acknowledge it, but with my departure from Exela inching ever closer, I wanted one last look at the place that decided my fate. Vines had crept up the walls and something had broken the windows. Curiosity overcame me and I peered inside, taking in the rotted wood furniture, moth-eaten blankets, and I could almost see the lonely little girl that lived there. It was too much, and I turned back to the path, walking briskly past Lys. Her mouth opened on a question; I didn't want to talk. We re-entered the house and as Lys locked the door, I felt something foreboding weigh me down like stones. As Lys bathed, I put away my jars, feeling relieved that although my hands and legs were tied up again that I could move around the room.

Lys escorted me down to the bathroom and looked away as I undressed and climbed into the bathtub. When I tapped on her with my hands, hoping she'd untie me, she shook her head.

"Come on! Haven't I proven that I'm not a threat? Do you know how hard it is to wash myself like this?" I shook my hands to make my point.

"Until you drink that tincture again and I know that I won't be killed, you'll be bound when out of my sight. But if it's too hard for you, I can always stay and help scrub you," she said, as she kneeled next to me and reached for the soap.

"Absolutely not!" I screamed and snatched the soap.

"I used to take baths with my female classmates all of the time, it's not like you have something I haven't seen."

"I don't care. You haven't seen my *things* before."

It wasn't until her smirk turned into an outright grin that I knew she was joking, and I felt the blush that formed across my cheeks travel down my body below the bubbles.

"Get out of here," I said, and splashed her as she stood up and walked away laughing.

"Fine, fine. I'll be in the kitchen, give a shout when you're ready to get out."

She left and I sunk down deeper into the bathtub, determined to soak for as long as possible. Lys confused me. She trusted me enough to wait in the kitchen, which was a few rooms down, but not enough to let me walk around freely. My fingers pruned so I gave in and scrubbed, trying to get the dirt out from my fingernails. As I lathered my hair and worked my fingers through the knots, I stopped. I heard something, but I couldn't figure where it came from. Rather than alerting Lys when it could just be a rat in the wall, I strained to hear it again.

With all the force of a thunderclap, the chorus erupted into my mind. The song! There it was! Oh, I didn't know how much I needed it until it was gone. The voices rose and fell, and I felt their longing and need for me just as bad as I longed and needed them. I needed them, my friends, my family, and they wanted, no, needed me to join them.

"Yessss," I hissed and climbed out.

The urgency flowing through them had me slipping out into the hall, water dripping down me to form puddles as I followed their voices. I reached the door that dared to separate us and tugged, so excited to embrace them and feel whole again! I'd been incomplete for so long. Too long. The door didn't move, and their song turned panicked, so we increased our efforts, and as I pulled, they pushed. *Thud, thud, thud,* the restraint of the door giving way a little bit more with every movement.

Chapter Ten — Lysandra

"Death. Death is the only goal of any necromancer. I began asking my necromancers why they did what they did. Why did they feel the need to attack humans when they could simply leave us alone. Their answer? The madness demanded more death. It needed to be fed souls. Necromancers are slaves to the madness; how could they refuse to add to the death toll when it commanded them to?"

—Braekios Journal #12, page 14

This had been a great day, the best I've had in a very long time. The lake was serene and for a little while I was able to forget why and who I was there with. All I felt was the not stale air flowing around me, and the scratch of sand beneath my feet. I was surprised when the necromancer answered my questions and even more surprised when it let me write its words down. I wasn't entirely sure what the Order was going to do with the necromancer when we made it back to Braeton, but I knew that its information was going to greatly expand the Order's understanding of the creatures. I was determined to use dinner to show it that although I had tied it up, I was beginning to trust it, a little bit. As I cooked the rabbit it would eat, keeping my nose closed, of course, I hummed a tune I learned from Dinah. Maybe I could get along with this necromancer after all. I'd still have to kill it in the end, but maybe we could be less hostile towards each other until then.

Something brushed up against my leg and I reached for my dagger before realizing it was Trickster.

"Hey, little fellow," I said and bent down to pet him. It wasn't until he started to purr that the blood drained from my face and into my toes, sending me staggering into the hallway.

"Shit," I told the newly awakened Trickster who trotted after me. Despite the smell of decay growing stronger each day, indicating the end of this experiment, I'd hoped that I'd have more time to figure out how I was going to introduce the necromancer to the Order.

I grabbed my dagger, hatchet, and brass knuckles from the chest I kept locked away in the bedroom before checking that the tincture was still safe in my pocket. I walked down the hall towards the thudding noise, loud and out of place in this normally quiet house. I rounded the corner and if the puddle of water I stepped in didn't cause me to fall on my ass, the sight in front of me would have.

I was used to the necromancer taking up little space in the house, and it usually chose to shrink in on itself instead of causing confrontation, but now, much like the first time we met, it commanded the space like a black hole, pulling in everything around it. Water still fell and I watched as drops traveled down the necromancer's soft form. I saw the tan lines that divided pale skin from areas bronzed by the sun, no doubt from spending so much time at the lake. Staring at its naked form, golden hair unbound and cascading down its body, the tips resting at its waist, and the eyes shining like a blade well-honed, I was reminded of the Fae heritage it fought to forget.

The door behind it slammed open and collapsed to the floor, the hinges pinging as they bounced across the floor and the corpses began to march out, two by two. My brain spun, frantically trying to come up with a plan that ended with my heart still beating. Running wasn't an option; I heard the corpses outside breaking down the front door and I knew it wasn't going to be long before they joined this fight.

"Feel the tincture wear off, my ass," I said, knowing that the necromancer wouldn't be able to hear me.

I needed to finish this fight quickly. I always trusted my gut to know what's best, so when it told me to forget the corpses and focus on getting to the necromancer, I took a step forward to start running. But my shock and planning cost me precious seconds and soon I faced off with the first two corpses out of the door. My heart broke to see that one was a young boy, now unfortunately stuck in the gangly years of puberty. It lunged towards me, and I pivoted, letting it move past my left side enough so that I could grab it by the hair and plant my hatchet into its throat with a powerful swing. I sawed off its head and let it fall to the floor, almost pulling me down with it. Again, I tried to run forward only to be yanked on my shoulder by a portly old dead man angling to take a bite of my neck. Its other hand angled for my eyes, but I managed to catch it and force the swollen fingers back into their joints. I winced as I heard them pop, knowing that they were broken, but the unfeeling corpse didn't hesitate to begin its next attempt at my neck. It leaned in again and I snatched the wrinkled face with both hands, wrenching it to a deadly angle.

Finally! Two down and a ton more to go. Great. While I fought for my life, more of the assholes paraded out of the room and formed a menacing and motley barricade between the necromancer and me.

"This is what happens when you get too comfortable," I grumbled to myself before I entered the killer's calm, which is what I should have done the second I saw the necromancer but was too distracted to do.

When I felt like a ripple on my mental lake instead of a wave, I looked for a way through the minefield. Not finding a path for me to weave through, I did what I do best and plowed forward, my hatchet swinging and my knuckles aching to feel bones crack beneath them. Fortunately for them, it wasn't long before I was attacked again. A pair of twins who were clearly blacksmiths lunged at me and managed to grab my arms, and turning from one to the other made me feel as if I had doubled my vision. Their grips felt like iron, and I knew that tugging free wasn't going to be an option. My arms being occupied meant I only had one option so I slammed my right heel, again encased in my trusty iron reinforced boots, into the top of the foot of the one holding my right hand. I hoped that the way his foot gave beneath mine would at least cause him to bend down, reacting to the pain, but this corpse was clearly a tree in a past life because he didn't even flinch. "Let's try this again," I thought before bringing my heel up and back into his knee. I gave this kick a little more *oompf* than the first, and luckily for me it was enough to hyper-extend his leg. He stumbled back, my foot helping send him on his way down. He hit the ground like a felled log, and I ripped my right hand free, feeling his nails dig into my skin as I did.

These twins were clearly as smart as stone, because the one who remained on his feet, my left arm still in his grasp, chose to look down at his fallen stump of a brother instead of me. I used his lack of knowledge of what not to do in a fight to slam my right fist, home of the very sadistic brass knuckles, into the nose of this other "previously a tree" corpse. My knuckles, satisfied for the second, left the corpse's face looking more like a freshly stepped-in cow turd than anything human, and the corpse fell to the floor, brain dead. A hand on my ankle reminded me there was still one of the brothers moving, and I heard Ms. Hannah chide me for making such a novice mistake. It tightened its grip and yanked me to the ground. As I lay on my back, hacking away at the corpse laying on top of me with my hatchet, I felt panic begin to return. My hatchet finally hit something vital and the hands reaching towards my face stilled. However, this corpse still laid on top of me, and his very large size left me scrambling to get out from underneath it.

My view of the necromancer disappeared as more and more corpses crowded my field of vision. I struggled to get back on my feet, only for a new corpse to push the deceased twin off me. I hoped to jump to my feet and face the new threat, but as I finally got to my knees something pushed me to the ground. I struggled to get back on my feet, pulling at the four sets of long, ruined fingernails digging into my arms and legs. This was not good, not good at all. My breath grew shaky, and I knew that my mental lake would be full of choppy waves. I twisted my head around and couldn't see anything beyond the dead and my own oncoming death. I needed a minute, no, a second, to calm down. I could spare a second, right? I couldn't die in a second. My eyes closed, I struggled to quickly settle my lake and reopened my eyes again, focus pushing away my trembling.

Luck must have been on my side because when I did open my eyes again, a window of opportunity appeared in the form of a face getting closer than it should. I threw my head forward with all my desperation, not caring that doing so brought my face within chomping range. The impact from our foreheads crashing together rattled my brain, but the corpse stumbled slightly, dropping my wrist as it stepped back. I channeled all my rage into ripping my still-restrained wrist free. Finally free of the dead girl's grasp, I grabbed her arms and threw her across my body, knocking down the corpse that was stepping back into place from its stumble. They both fell in a tangle of limbs. Sitting up quickly, I leaned forward to the feet of the dead teenager that stood there, sluggishly reacting to my freedom. My dagger was in my hand before I knew it and I used it to slice the teen's tendons, wincing slightly as he collapsed on the ground. One corpse remained leering at me, but I was finally capable of standing up to take it on. I rose to a kneeling position, grabbed its head, and brought it into the sharp bone of my knee. It collided with a crunch, and I twisted the head, ensuring that it would never rise again.

I felt a moment of joy at being back on my feet, only to feel my heart sink at the amount of corpses that I had to navigate to reach the necromancer. There was a loud crash behind me, and I didn't need to turn my head to know that the remaining dead outside had finally broken down the door and joined the fight. Great, that was fucking great, screw the fighting, I needed to reach the necromancer. Force its mouth open, uncork the tincture mid-struggle, and force it to swallow the liquid I poured down its throat. All while dodging creatures that didn't understand personal space. Okay, that was a lot of justs, but I told myself that it was all doable. I shoved, ducked, and jumped my way to the necromancer, feeling wounds open on my arms and legs, the blood loss starting to make me dizzy. I didn't take my eyes off the necromancer, and I knew that the lack of awareness I had of my surroundings would cost me in the end, probably in the form of new scars added to my growing collection.

I couldn't decide if the fuzzy blackness at the edge of my vision was because of the tunnel vision or served as a warning sign that I soon would be unconscious, but it didn't matter, because with one last shove through arms that grabbed me, I reached the necromancer. Panting, I grabbed its head, forced it under my arm, and much like you would do with a dog chewing on something it shouldn't, pried the mouth open with one hand and poured the tincture that I had thumbed open with the other. I held its mouth and nose shut until I knew that the tincture was swallowed. The seconds seemed long, and I hoped that the tincture worked against this large army, because I lied. It wasn't a lot of justs, it was too many. Already I saw more of the dead outside climbing in through the windows, glass tinkling as it fell to the floor, and I was out of plans. They got closer and the pounding of my heart drowned out any other sounds. This was going to be my tomb, I knew it, and I wondered what it would feel like to have an afterlife. The necromancer stopped struggling under my arm and it took me a minute to register the plop of falling bodies.

"Lys?" I heard a quiet voice and looked down to see the necromancer's eyes, still bright but without the cruelty they had seconds ago. With a haunted expression on its face, it whispered, "You can let me go. I'm back, well, not to normal, but back to myself."

It held still until I loosened my hold.

"Oh, good." I barely got the words out before the blackness claimed me.

Chapter Eleven — Lysandra

"We will go wherever we are needed. I will establish a network of communication so that when an attack happens, we can respond in whatever way is needed. We will rebuild towns, burn the deceased, and kill the necromancer responsible."

—Braekios Journal #10, page 56

"If I ever wake up on this table again, it will be too soon. You couldn't put me on a bed? Come on, my back's going to be killing me all week," I croaked out upon waking up on the damned table, again. I looked for the necromancer and found it sitting in the familiar spot next to me. It had its elbows on its lap, hands holding its head as it peered at me.

"At least you're not tied up this time. Though if you'd prefer that, I'm sure I could find some more ropes somewhere," it joked weakly, concern tugging the corner of its lips down, before gently helping me into a sitting position.

I noticed white bandages wrapped around my arms, down my body, and even one on my left foot. "How long was I out?" I peered closer at the ones on my hand, there was a pungent smell coming from it. "What the fuck did you put on me? Because it smells like shit and I'm really hoping it's not."

The necromancer chuckled slightly and peeled back the bandages to look closer at the wounds. She nodded, happy at the progress with which my wounds were healing.

"It's been twenty-six hours. You needed your rest, so I didn't try waking you. Though considering how still you were, I'm not sure if I could have woken you up, you were more in a comatose state than a restful sleep. As for what's on you, it's not shit, but you don't want to know what it is. I added something to it to expedite the healing, but the smell can be alarming."

It grew quiet and its hands gripped mine, causing my knuckles to throb again. "Thank you, Lys. You had plenty of reasons to kill me, but you didn't."

The way the silver eyes stared into mine made me shift uncomfortably.

"We made a deal; I wasn't going to back out of it. Plus, the knowledge you possess is way more important than another dead necromancer."

"Would another necromancer bandage your wounds, and ensure your safety? Because I knew humans wouldn't have done for you what I did. After everything I've done for you, am I still another monster for you to kill?"

The tears gathering at it... Her eyes, and the vulnerability that I saw pulled at my soul. This wasn't another necromancer, this was Talia, a person who had been working to make the world a better place despite the hardship and struggles she'd encountered... Like me. If I had taken the time to talk to the necromancers I fought, learned more about who they were as a person, could I have helped them? Could we have worked together to understand how to live peacefully? Damn it, my head throbbed too much for me to think about these kinds of things.

"You're not a monster, Talia."

As I said her name, she offered a watery smile. "I'm not?"

"No, you're not. You haven't killed anyone; you've dedicated your life to find a way to gain control over something that others in the same situation embrace. You say I had plenty of reasons to kill you, but I could say the same thing about you. You could've killed me the first day we met or when I lay on your table again. Instead, you tended to my wounds, and remained civil with me, even when I threatened your life. Multiple times. That's not something that a monster does."

She laughed and I couldn't resist reaching forward to wipe away her tears, the softness of her cheek brushing against my callused finger.

"What comes next?" She asked, her voice a little steadier than it was seconds ago.

"We go to the Order, and you teach them how to make Philipa's Tincture. Imagine the good it could do if we could distribute it, or weaponize it. With the increase in necromantic strength we've been encountering recently, we'll need all the help we can get."

"Wait." Talia's voice was hesitant. "How have necromancers become more powerful?

"We're not too sure, but the last few that were killed were recorded as mentioning something called Nectar."

At the mention of Nectar, her mouth fell open and quickly snapped close again. "I'm not too sure, but I think Nectar has to do with blood." Her fingers traced a long scratch on her arm that was almost healed.

"Why would you think that?"

She grasped her arm, hiding most of the scratch, and told me about how exactly she came to be in control of so many bodies.

"All the more reason to go to the Order! They need to know about this, and maybe they can figure out what makes your blood so special."

She shook her head. "I'm not going to the Order, not anymore."

"What do you mean? When we met you convinced me that you wanted to go. That was the only reason that I didn't kill you."

Her voice was cold when she said, "That was before I knew how widespread Nectar was and how crucial my blood is to it. I'm not about to go and offer myself up as a guinea pig so that the Order can figure out exactly how to use me. I can only imagine what kind of methods your

Order will use to get my blood. I'm sorry Lys, I like my life, I don't want to spend the rest of my days chained up, anemic, and squinting at the sun as it comes through a tiny window in my cell."

She was about to walk out of the room before I managed to swing off the table, which pulled a grunt out of me, and grab her wrist. Her heartbeat fluttered beneath my fingers, and I could feel how afraid she was. Whatever this Nectar was, the idea of it scared her enough into wanting to hide away from the world.

"You will not end up in the cells, nor as the Order's plaything. I will keep you safe, and free. I promise you this." I held her eyes as my voice turned pleading, I needed her to believe me, to see that the knowledge and skills she offered outweighed the risk of being locked away. "Please Talia, what you know could change the tides of the battle against necromancy. You love to help people; don't you see all the good you could do by coming with me to the Order? I… Swear on my life." I dropped her hand and pulled out my dagger. I didn't hesitate to let myself think about what I was doing before slicing a deep cut on my right arm. Blood oaths weren't really used anymore, mainly due to the risk of the infection, but Braekios believed that a necromancer wouldn't willingly give away their blood, so it was created as a sign of loyalty, faith, and that the person taking it was fully human. There was one member, a young man jealous of the power that Braekios had, who gave away their location to a necromancer with a grudge. Enough of the Order escaped, including Braekios, on his deathbed due to the blood disease he'd inadvertently given himself, to continue. But of the ones who died, that chasseur was the last one, and it's said that his blood boiled in his veins, death coming to him because of his betrayal of the blood oath. The legend formed around this, and most people believed that a blood oath couldn't be broken. I wasn't sure I believed that, but I did recognize the power of symbolism and I hoped that Talia knew enough of the legend to put her faith and trust in me.

Her eyes widened in alarm at the blood dripping down my forearm, and I spoke again. "I, Lysandra Spits, swear on my life that I will keep you alive and out of harm." My eyes beseeched her. Please, let that be enough. If Talia demanded my life in payment for her going to the Order, I'd gladly give it. The Order has plenty of people like me, but Talia was like a comet, something that only came once every few lifetimes.

She closed her eyes briefly and sighed. "Great, now I have another wound that I need to tend to. Fine." She took the dagger from me and sliced open the almost healed cut on her left arm. "I, Talia Ashowen, accept your vow. If I harm you or your people outside of self-defense, the vow and my life are forfeit."

She grasped my elbow and I swear I felt our blood dancing as we pressed our wounds together.

"Let's get these cleaned up and bandaged."

Dinner that night was a feast. Since our plan was to travel to Braeton tomorrow, we cooked anything that would spoil during our trip, and I swear that the enticing aromas could've brought anyone back to life. I gave Talia a crash course on how to pack and we spent the rest of the evening sorting through things that we would and wouldn't be bringing with us. Crouching down frequently to pick and pack things had my body growing stiff, so we went to bed early, with the intention of leaving with the rising sun. I'd never slept that well in my life. Without the stress of the week hanging over me, and my body still tired from the fight, the moment I put my head down, I was asleep, the nightmares that normally plagued me blissfully absent.

The next morning, I awoke to Talia gently shaking me awake, and when she noticed that I looked up at her with eyes still fogged over from sleep, she backed away.

"Good morning," my voice still rough from the hold my slumber had on me. Clearing my throat to rid myself of the night's sleep, I noticed that she was fully dressed, and sunlight poured in through the window, warming the stone floor beneath my feet. "Damn, I didn't mean to oversleep, I don't even remember the last time I did that."

Her twinkling laugh followed her as she walked over to the window and opened it to allow a crisp breeze to chase out the stagnant bedroom air.

"You're still healing, you needed the sleep, and I wasn't going to wake you until I knew that you weren't going to wake up on your own. I have breakfast waiting in the kitchen, get changed quickly so we can eat it before it grows cold." She left, closing the door behind her.

Talia claimed that she had wanted to say goodbye to the house, so I ate the still warm breakfast alone, inhaling the food in my eagerness to get on the road and return home. I found Talia outside the front door that still hung off its hinges from the attack, staring at the house with a solemn expression.

"There's something I need to do before we leave. I know it's going to set us back, but I wouldn't feel comfortable leaving without doing this first." Before I was able to ask what that thing was, she continued. "The people of Exela deserve a proper burial. They helped me when I needed them most, and I've kept them trapped here in their afterlives, when they should've been allowed to move on. I've spent most of my life here, but now that chapter of my life is as dead as they are, and it deserves a proper ending too."

It wasn't until she brought branches over that I understood what she was going to do, and I helped her drag over large logs and kindling. We lit the fire and watched as it quickly ate the dry wood, the flames reaching towards the wood of the house and the contents inside it.

We were silent, and I jumped when she spoke at last, her voice husky, and I knew she was fighting the emotions that must have been forming in her throat. "Thank you, Lani, Genfry, Richard…" The list went on and on, but I stayed silent, knowing first hand that saying goodbye helped heal the wounds the past inflicts.

The names slowed down after I counted two-hundred-and-four. At the name, "Imogene…" Her voice caught and I saw the glimmer of tears making her eyes sparkle more than normal. "Trickster. You all raised me. While you caused me pain there were good moments too, and you've shaped me into the woman I am today. Your names, and your stories, will stay engraved on my heart."

She turned, at last, and walked away from her home and everyone she knew, not looking back except to usher me forward with a small jerk of her head towards the road. Helpless to do anything, and unsure of what, if anything I could say, I followed her. With Talia leaving Exela it officially became a ghost town, and I credited the loss to the necromantic struggle. Places like here and Qui would stay empty and haunted until some adventurous people decided to make it home again, but that would only happen when the tale of what happened was forgotten.

We walked for a few hours before the night made it too difficult to see. While I was used to traveling through the darkness and could go on for a few more hours, the sound of Talia's stumbling footsteps had me leading her off the road and to a grassy spot to set up camp. We quietly ate a meal of bread, water, and root vegetables, and laid down to rest, the stars barely visible through the canopy of leaves above us. Talia was quiet, and just as I was sure she was asleep, she spoke. "What does the Order believe happens to us once we die?" Her voice was shy, and I could tell she was worried about offending me with the question.

I didn't have to think long before formulating my response. "Braekios, the founder of the Order, believed in science above all else. Officially the Order doesn't believe in anything. When a person dies, their bodies are burned and the ashes feed the plants, and that's it." I hesitated, not used to talking about my feelings. "Personally, I think we go to the stars, to watch over the ones who remain, and guide us when we need it. That they're saying hi to us every time the stars twinkle in the night sky, letting us know that we're not alone."

I heard a rustle and saw that Talia had curled in on herself. "I like that. Imogene was more of a mother to me than my own mother was, it's nice to think that she's still watching over me." Speaking of her past seemed to awaken something within her and she laughed. "She'd like you," she said matter-of-factly.

"Oh yeah? Why's that?"

"You speak your mind. She never liked the word-smithing people did. Say what you mean, she'd tell me anytime I'd tiptoe around what I really wanted to say. She gave me a chance, like you. She could've run away screaming when she first saw my eyes. She could've killed me any day she wanted. Instead, she invited me into her home, and taught me everything she knew. When I gave into the madness she didn't cower, she made sure I was safe from myself and from the townspeople."

"She sounds like an incredible person."

"She was." That was the end of the conversation. Talia's breath grew slow and even and I knew that she'd finally fallen asleep.

I stared up at the stars, and as they twinkled, I smiled. "Hey Dinah, I know that I've made some mistakes, but I hope you can see that this is not one of them."

That night I dreamed of Braeton and introduced Talia to it. In my mind, I watched as she looked at the city with wonder and ate all my favorite foods greedily, enjoying every second of it. She, Niamh, Dinah and I went to the tavern together and spent the night laughing and drinking. There was a sense of peace within my heart, and I knew that she would fit right in, her research etched into the tomes that would be used to teach future generations.

Chapter Twelve — Talia

"Necromancers have enhanced senses, no doubt inherited from their Fae lineage, and their sense of smell is extraordinarily strong. I have watched a necromancer travel miles to the corpse it scented, undeterred by the smells of human towns or the winds that scatter the smell."

—Braekios Journal #4, page 12

Everything was in pain. My back hurt. My feet hurt. Even my wrists hurt. Waking up, I quickly decided that I didn't enjoy sleeping on grass, no matter how plush it looked. I turned to tell Lys as much, but the smile on her face and the gleam in her eyes had me swallowing my remark.

"I should've known you were an outdoorsy person when you dove into that freezing cold lake," I grumbled, standing up and stretching my arms above my head in hopes of alleviating some of the stiffness in my body.

I saw her eyes flick to the exposed part of my stomach as my shirt rode up a little bit and watched as her ear turned pink before she returned to stomping out the fire. That was odd, but I was too preoccupied with today's march to think too hard about it.

"There's something so freeing about the outdoors," Lys said. "Everything's so simple here. There aren't any protocols for me to follow, no one to receive orders from, just fresh air."

"And bugs." I smacked at a fly that landed on my arm.

She cocked her head at me.

"What?" I wasn't sure that I liked the way she studied me.

"You weren't this… Outspoken in Exela."

"I was afraid that I was one wrong word away from meeting the sharp point of your dagger."

She grinned and my eyes caught on the dimples I hadn't noticed before. "I'm super glad that you didn't."

"Me too."

There was an awkward beat between us, both of us clearly unsure of what to say next.

I worked my fingers through the knots in my hair. "What's the plan? We walk until our feet leave us behind?"

This was going to be my first adventure without Mom, and I was determined to make the best of it, no matter what the destination may hold for me. As we packed our things back up, I listened to Lys excitedly explain the path we were taking.

Seemed like we'd stay under the canopy of the forest until we reached Noxid, which marked the halfway point to Braeton. I fumbled through my pack, searching for the one thing that would make walking through this bug-infested humidity bearable. I found my bug repellent balm and slathered it onto any exposed skin.

"Here." I passed it to Lys. "Put this on. I made it so that the mosquitoes wouldn't drive me insane while I was at the lake."

She sniffed it and coughed. "If it's as strong as it smells, we'll be clear of bugs for hundreds of miles."

Once our campsite was clear of any markings that we'd been there, I followed behind Lys, keeping one eye on her and one eye on the plants around me. I recognized many of them, but didn't need them, so I just admired their tenacity to thrive. As we walked further and further from Exela, I recognized less and tried my best to memorize their appearances so that I could do more research once we had a break. I didn't bring all the books that were in the house, but I brought several large encyclopedias that would be put to good use as I came across new flora and fauna. When Lys passed back a sandwich for lunch and kept walking it became apparent that we'd spend the whole day walking. As the day passed, I felt my feet rubbing against my shoes through the softness of my socks. Eventually, not even the occasional pretty flower could distract me from the pain, and I fell even further behind Lys, my hobbling steps preventing me from catching up.

When that hobble became a limp, and that limp became a drag, I knew that I wasn't going to be able to continue.

"I need a break," I said, hoping Lys was close enough to hear me.

I sat on a rock, not waiting for a response, and peeled the layers of socks and shoes off my feet.

When Lys saw the blood soaking through my sock, she sucked air in through her teeth. "Why didn't you say something sooner?" Her hands were gentle and steady on my feet as she looked at the blisters that decorated both heels.

"I know we're in a hurry. I didn't want to slow us down." I fished out my salve and went to apply it, only for Lys to take it from me and apply it herself.

When I hissed in pain, she said, "That's ridiculous. I want to get there as soon as possible, but not at the risk of you hurting yourself."

With bandages applied to both feet and socks switched out, I went to put on my shoes, anticipating that we'd begin walking again, but instead let out a yelp of surprise when Lys scooped me up into her arms.

"I can walk, you know! Put me down."

"Nope. If we keep going now, they'll reopen and hurt even worse. We'll settle down near here for the night and start back up in the morning."

She swung me over her shoulder and left the road to find a spot that was flat and sheltered from the wind that started to pick up. The sun set but there was still plenty of light left, so I leafed through the few books I packed, looking for the plants I came across but didn't have a name for while Lys started a fire. There was a briskness in the air that spoke of a cold night ahead of us and I pulled out my additional layers to put on to help me stay warm.

Dinner was slightly stale bread, more root vegetables, and water. We sat close to the fire and enjoyed the stillness around us. I watched as the flames danced in the reflection of Lys's hazel eyes and realized that I was desperate to know more about the place I was soon going to call home.

"What's Braeton like? That's where the Order is, right?" I was apparently not as good at hiding my apprehension as I thought because Lys smirked before sliding closer to me, our knees touching ever so slightly.

"Well," she began, a far off look in her eyes. "Braeton may be called a city, but you'd never know it by looking at it. The whole city's built into the hills, and the buildings often blend in, with most mimicking the hills and grassy areas around it. The doors, on the other hand, are usually painted in vibrant colors, anything from red to sky blue or fuschia. From a distance, they almost look like wildflowers. The roads wind around the hills which means that it can take hours to travel a short distance. Most people choose to hike up the steps built into the hillsides with their bags instead of waiting for a wagon to bring them up. The Order headquarters sit on the highest hill, so high up that you feel as though you're in the clouds. You wouldn't believe the number of times I've had to run up and down that hill for punishment."

She spoke late into the night, both of us laying down under our blankets, staring up at the stars, which seemed brighter than normal thanks to the new moon. I fell asleep during a story of the time she and her friends decided to roll down the hill inside one of the giant barrels the Order used to store water.

Without knowing how much time passed, I startled awake, and it took me a minute to realize that it was Lys's hand on my mouth that woke me, her eyes urgent as she leaned down to whisper, "Something's watching us."

I gulped and my eyes darted to the trees around us, but the clouds covered the starlight, making the darkness so complete that I couldn't see anything beyond the low flames of the fire we slept next to. I felt, rather than saw, Lys slowly pull out her weapons as she stood up.

"Look," she said with a cocky smile, slowly spinning her hatched in a tight circle. "I know you're there, and we both know that I know. Why don't you stop wasting time that we could be using to sleep and come on out? It's way too late to be awake and I'd like to get some more rest before the sun comes out."

I started to stand up but froze at the laugh coming from somewhere within the trees outside our campsite. "Aren't you perceptive," the voice purred, clearly female. There was a sound of several feet crunching down on twigs and I immediately knew two things. One—the person approached us, and two, they weren't alone. By the way Lys's hands gripped her hatchet and brass knuckles harder, I knew that she figured it out, too.

"How many of you are there?" Lys asked, throwing her voice around us.

The person didn't respond to Lys but did say, "He was right! When Luther said he found someone whose blood smelled like Nectar, I thought he was lying. But I've used enough of it to know what it smells like, and I decided to see if I could track it down. You wouldn't believe how much time I spent wandering around. But it was worth it!" She suddenly appeared to my left and

I jumped at her quiet approach. I saw her violet eyes examining me before she inhaled my scent. "Here you are, my personal Nectar supply!"

Lys took two small but decisive steps, placing herself between me and the necromancer.

"I don't like the way you've been speaking about my friend here." Lys pointed her hatched at the necromancer and slid her right foot back into a fighting stance. "Why don't you leave the way you came? I'd hate for you to find out what happens if you decide to stick around."

No response came from the necromancer except to slink forward, her steps light and quick. I heard a snap behind me and whirled around to see a pack of starved-looking wolves staring at me, their unblinking eyes reflecting by the flames.

"Lys." I whispered, tugging on her sleeve slightly. There was no way we could fight them all.

"I know," she whispered back. "How did you get these wolves under your control? I didn't even know that Hawk's Forrest had wolves," she said to the necromancer while pulling out the dagger still tucked away and shoving it into my hands.

She had a good point, though. I knew necromancy was powerful, but I had a hard time believing that the skinny young woman in front of me could overpower and kill the wolves that surrounded us. Her clothes were practically rags and she smelled as if she hadn't bathed in years.

"Nectar made it all too easy. With it inside me, I needed no food, nor water. I waited, playing dead for a week, until the wolves wandered over in search of their next meal. I ripped out the heart of the closest one with my bare hands." She held her hands out as if we could still see the blood on them. "Once it died, I brought it back to life and made it slaughter its pack mates. I'm going to watch them kill you." She pointed a finger at Lys. "And drag you away with me."

She swung the finger to where I stood. "There's someone that would be very interested in meeting you." I had no idea who that person may have been, but I knew it was not someone I wanted to meet.

I saw Lys close her eyes and take a deep breath before going completely still. The necromancer sensed an opportunity and sent a wolf leaping towards me with the dying fire glinting off its sharp teeth. Lys's eyes sprang open and as she turned towards the lunging wolf she whipped her hatchet up, slicing through its head. The body collapsed inches away from where I cowered, and she pulled me in close to her.

"Stay behind me, and keep that dagger pointed away from me. If one gets past me, jab it with the pointy end. I trust you know which end that is." I nodded and she exhaled, "Good," before taking another deep breath and stepping towards the wolves, putting the necromancer, who was the bigger threat, but not the most immediate one, behind her.

I held the dagger out in front of me and watched the necromancer for any sort of signs that she was going to attack us herself, but instead she laughed, saying, "I have no need of attacking you myself when these dogs can do it for me. I'll be back to collect you once your will to fight is gone," before disappearing into the darkness she came from.

Out of the corner of my eye I saw five wolves form a semicircle around Lys who side-stepped their snapping jaws. Reaching out, she landed a punch that cracked on impact across the jaw of one that leaned in to bite at her legs. The impact from the hit sent it falling to the ground and Lys spun around to kill another one that approached me.

She caught me watching her and gave me a glare, reminding me to trust her to fight the ones in front of her, and that it was my duty to alert her to the ones, like this one, that had snuck around me. The bodies slowly piled up with every jab of her fist and swing of her hatchet. One leaped towards her, and I watched as she ducked underneath it, swinging her hatchet up as she did so, slicing it in two before it landed on the ground. I held the dagger and tried to focus on anything besides the work of art that fought at my side, but my eyes continued to drift to Lys.

There was no energy wasted, each step she took was efficient and graceful. Her hands followed the most direct path and her knuckles always hit their intended target. As I contemplated the weird mixture of awe, gratitude, and lust that I felt watching her, more wolves advanced on Lys and my breaths turned shallow, fearing that she'd be overwhelmed. I looked at the dagger in my hand. Could I help her? No, I decided quickly, not with this. I sank to the ground, placing the dagger nearby before reaching for my pack that was still in its original spot. I fished out the mosquito repellent and pulled out a glob of the balm before rolling it in the dry grass. Back on my feet, I pulled a smoldering stick from the fire and used it to light my makeshift bomb. I quickly lobbed it at the wolves that watched the fight from the back of the pack, waiting their turn to strike. While I was concerned about the wolves currently engaging Lys, I was more afraid of accidentally hitting her. The bomb hit the wolves and immediately burned away at the wolves' fur like a flame ate at dry kindling. The smoldering furs brought the fight into clearer view, and it seemed as if every living and undead thing paused to look at me.

"What the fuck was that?!" Lys panted. I felt pride swell in my heart at the way I was able to help, not by doing what I was told, but on my own terms.

I shrugged, trying to come across as nonchalant. "The ingredients I used in the bug repellent are highly flammable. That's why I keep it in an airtight container."

"That was fucking awesome! Keep it up!"

I pretended the heat in my face was from my proximity to the fire and not due to her praise. I quickly made five slightly smaller bombs and watched as the flames burned away first the fur, and then the fat and bones. For once, fighting a dead enemy worked in my favor, as it meant that they felt no pain as they slowly burned to death, choosing to continue the fight instead of rolling in the dirt to put out the flames that destroyed them. Slowly, so slowly, the wolves burned to ash. Lys jumped on the back of the last wolf, a massive beast that must've been the alpha, and it fell to the floor attempting to roll and throw Lys free.

She slowly slipped off but got her hatchet up at an angle that had me wincing in sympathetic pain, and wedged it into the head, waiting for the body to stop twitching before getting up again. With that last wolf dead, we turned to the necromancer who… Was no longer there, great.

"Shit, she got away," Lys panted, sweat, blood and other gore dripping off her in steaming chunks. "There's no way we can catch her without any light. I may be good at tracking, but I'm not that good," she said as I wandered around and took inventory of the casualties to our stuff.

Our packs survived, but our sleeping pads were both ripped to shreds, no doubt courtesy to sharp claws on big paws. I wasn't looking forward to having nothing to separate me from the things that crawled on the ground while I slept.

"Should we try to go back to sleep for a little while longer?" Lys asked, toeing the remains of our sleeping pads, but the woods were slowly coming to life, full of the morning bird's song. Lys followed my gaze up to the sky of pinks and rosy reds and shrugged. "Early start so we can relax longer when we get to Noxid?"

We began to walk, again. I was getting tired of walking, but right before I decided that it couldn't get any worse, I felt a few giant cold drops of rain slide down my arms and face. It rained all day and every step I took had my shoes squelching in a sound I decided was the exact song of misery. My teeth chattered, and my hands were incapable of rubbing any warmth into my arms and fingers. I could almost have believed that Lys was unaffected by the rain if it weren't for the frequent full body shivers I witnessed traveling through her body. My nose ran, and the combination of snot and rain had me on the verge of reaching for one of my more lethal concoctions when I saw the alluring light of Noxid shining through the trees like a beacon. I tripped over my feet in my eagerness to get inside a cozy tavern and Lys helped me back up before attempting to brush off some of the mud that clung to me.

"Almost there," she said before picking up the pace, clearly as in need of a dry place as me.

We reached Noxid twenty minutes later and looked for our destination, though we didn't have to look too hard. Noxid was less of a town and more of a place. The dirt road rose and fell into deep holes as it creeped around the wooden houses scattered about. The houses slumped in on themselves as if the rain was slowly bringing them to the ground and the grayness of the fog seemed to be at home here, making me believe that Noxid would be dull and faded even without the rain.

The Weary Traveller's Rest was the only inn that also served as Noxid's only tavern. Despite the incessant rain and the early hour, there were still some local drunks standing under the awning, passing a jug around that they took long swigs of. When they weren't drinking. they spat something thick out through the gap in their teeth or were pulling something out of a torn pocket on drab clothes that were ill-fitting. As we approached the door below the crooked sign proclaiming its name along with a rough drawing of a sleeping man, I caught a whiff of body odor, alcohol and the smell unique to lack of showering, while feeling a pinch on my behind that was sudden and strong. I heard the snickers follow me, but Lys ushered me inside before I was able to turn around and scold the cretin that did it. My ears burned red, but judging by the way those laughs abruptly stopped, Lys must have given them one of her looks that guaranteed death.

Inside the Weary Traveller's Rest was more of the same, a sea of gray, smelly people sitting around small, unsteady, sticky tables in desperate need of being cleaned. The walls were white once but were now some weird shades of mildew with crooked paintings of landscapes placed sporadically about. The pictures desperately tried to bring a little life to the inn, showing images of forest in the full embrace of spring, the ocean under a clear sunny day, and snow covering the rooftops of a little town, but they all seemed to fade into the grayness of the wall, giving the place the feeling of something that had been washed so many times it lost any luster it may have had.

Across from the door we entered was the bar, long and precarious-looking. A large woman with wiry black hair and a caterpillar for eyebrows stood behind it, polishing the counter with a filthy brown rag. She was entirely focused on her task and didn't look up when we sat on rickety chairs in front of her. It took Lys clearing her throat twice for her to sigh and drag her attention to us.

"What can I get ya?" She asked, leaning forward to prop an elbow on the bar.

"Two rooms please," Lys said, offering the woman way more courtesy than she'd been giving us.

"Does it look like I've got two rooms to spare?" Was the sarcastic response we received along with a gesture to the people milling around.

I turned to take in the tables fully occupied by worn-out people, where some chattered or played cards but most drank deeply from their mismatched tankards.

"No?" I responded, hoping it was the right answer.

The barkeep grunted and fished out a warped key from the pocket in her apron. She slammed it onto the table saying, "I've got one left. Twenty coppers."

My eyes widened, there was no way any room in this establishment was worth that much, but Lys clearly didn't care. "We'll take it! Anything's better than camping out in the rain."

With the payment received we were told dinner started at seven, breakfast started at six, and were given a gesture to the vague direction of our room. We walked up creaky stairs and past rooms that emitted noises causing me to blush deeply before reaching our room.

As expected, the room wasn't worth the twenty coppers. It was bare, with a roof that dripped water into a bucket placed in the middle of the room, a small, dusty uneven desk with an equally small chair and a small lantern placed on it with a match to light the fuse when we needed it. The bed tucked in the corner was the most lavish piece in the room, with a blanket that looked in need of a washing but seemed soft and two pillows. I couldn't wait to drop my things and fall into it. I'd actively been avoiding looking in the bathroom, and when I opened the door, I immediately regretted it. A large pot and pitcher of cold water served as the sink, but more alarming was the lack of a proper toilet. Growing up in several towns, I knew that having indoor plumbing was a luxury, but I had grown used to having it in Exela. The toilet, unfortunately, was an enclosure with a seat and a bucket precariously attached to it. There was a sign next to it stating to leave our waste in front of the door before morning to be cleaned. I quickly closed the door and gulped, watching Lys inspect the mattress.

She saw my questioning look and said, "I've stayed in a lot of places like this. Trust me, there's nothing worse than waking up to bug bites. You can usually find them crawling around. But," the mattress was thrown back on the frame, "we lucked out! I don't see any of those little shits."

She sat down on it with a sigh and massaged her neck. I joined her and was relieved to feel that the mattress was not as firm as it appeared.

"What do we do now?" There wasn't a lot for us to do and the last thing I wanted to do was watch the water slowly drip into the bucket. "Given our early morning start I'm definitely in need of a nap."

Lys was already tucked underneath the blankets, having snuggled into the bed by the time I said "nap". I looked to the floor, torn between sleeping on the hard floor or next to Lys before I was quickly pulled down, the decision out of my hands.

"I don't bite, promise." Lys murmured before turning over to face the wall and fell asleep. I lay there, rigid, listening to the way Lys breathed next to me, certain that there was no way I was going to be able to sleep and yet finding my thoughts drift the way they do before you fall asleep.

A door closed loudly somewhere down the hall, and I was ripped from my slumber. Trying to sit up became impossible when I noticed that sometime during our nap, long given the way the rain had stopped and the sun was well past its rising stage, Lys had entwined herself with me. Her arm rested across my stomach, and I had to fish my hand out from beneath her head, being careful not to disturb her. I shouldn't have tried though, because as soon as I shifted my weight to get out her eyes opened and focused on mine. She sat up and stretched, not noticing how rigid I was. "Man, I'm hungry! Guess we slept through lunch time." She pulled out a well-loved deck of cards. "Fancy an early dinner and game or two?"

I nodded, hoping she didn't talk about the way I was curled into her seconds ago, and we walked past the noisy rooms and back down to the main room. Food was a watery cabbage soup with chunks of chicken and slightly stale bread on the side. It wasn't good, but it was warm, and after walking through the rain all day, that was all that mattered.

Our bellies full and cups of beer sitting next to us, Lys explained the rules of the game. "It's a pattern, Death," she held up a card with a skull on it, "Rebirth," a flower blooming, "Lust," two figures intertwined, "Love," two birds in flight, "and Life," a tree with its branches reaching to the sky. "When it's your turn, flip over a card and say the next word in the pattern. If the word matches the card, you slap the pile. The last person to slap takes the deck and drinks. If you flinch or slap when you shouldn't, you take the deck and drink. The first one with no cards wins. Ready?"

I nodded and she split the deck of cards in half. We gathered the cards in our hands and began the game.

"Life!" I said and slapped the card, Lys's hand touching it a fraction too late. She shook her head and took a long drink.

We played a while longer until Lys made a comeback and was down to one card. She flipped it over saying, "Rebirth" and we both went to slap the pile, my hand resting on hers instead of the cards. My thumb brushed gently over her knuckles before I could stop myself and I jerked it away when I realized that Lys had gone still below my touch.

"Don't feel too bad," Lys said as I finished off my drink. "I played this growing up. There's no way you could've beat me."

"Plus, I seem to have the reflexes of a slug," I sighed, and Lys laughed.

Flagging down the innkeeper/bartender (we found out her name was Bertilda) to get another round of drinks, I declared, "This is going to be the round I beat you."

We played late into the night, the rain resuming its deluge, the crowd around us dwindling down to the few who decided it was easier to fall asleep on the table than make their way home. I lost game after game, never getting close to winning, and after the first three of my losses Lys decided to drink whenever I drank, deeming it unfair if she didn't. But with every sip of my drink, I cared less and less about winning and was more interested in the way Lys's eyelashes brushed her cheek as she glanced down.

The cry of, "Last call! Get your drink and get out!" From Bertilda had us cleaning up the game and heading back to our room. It was hard to tell if I leaned on Lys or if she leaned on me, but we managed to stumble upstairs and into our room.

We changed into our night clothes, back-to-back, when the room began to spin. My shirt was on, but as I tried to pull up my pants, my foot got tangled in them and I fell to the floor, landing painfully on my butt. At the sound of my swearing, Lys whirled around, her eyes a little unfocused but trying their best to assess the threat. She wore what she always did to bed, a simple breast band and the shorts that were so worn they were almost see-through.

She laughed seeing my face pinched in drunken anger at gravity and bent down, offering a hand to help me up. I clung to it and slowly stood up only to feel the world spin once again and yanked Lys down to the floor with me. She landed painfully on her ass too and I watched as she registered her new position on the floor rather than where she stood seconds ago. The confusion on her face was too much and I laughed, Lys joining in. We inched to rest our backs against the edge of the bed and continued to laugh, drunk from the beer and on the sensation of being dry and out of danger. We laughed until tears fell down our faces and our cheeks hurt from smiling. My head found its way onto Lys's shoulder and while she hesitated at first, she slowly ran her hand through my hair, gently working through the knots she encountered. My eyes fluttered closed and I moved in closer, encouraged by her unsteady breath, wanting to hear her heartbeat and feel her beneath me.

"I've never seen hair like yours," she whispered, her lips pressed against the top of my head.

"Mm," I said in response, content to feel the rumble of her voice travel through my body. Her hand worked its way slowly down to the tips of my hair then to my shoulder, slowing as it traveled down to my exposed thigh, and I stiffened, knowing what she saw there.

"What are these from?" She asked, brushing her thumb over one of the raised scars that formed neat little lines on both of my thighs. "I would say that you got them in a fight, I have plenty of those, but these are too organized, too straight."

I wished she hadn't seen those, but I wasn't ashamed of my past and I told her the truth. "When my mom left, I didn't have anyone or anywhere to go, so my teacher, Imogene, took me in. She taught me everything I know and helped me to learn to see my powers as a gift instead of a curse. I was happy, for once, learning and serving as her assistant. But then came the wet sickness."

I took a shuddering breath and willed myself to go on. Lys didn't say anything, but I felt her hand on my thigh squeeze it gently, telling me to take my time. "A lot of people got sick, and we were busy helping people pass on and making the ones on their way out more comfortable. It was hard, hard, and I took Philipa's Tincture every day, in fear of slipping up. Imogene caught the sickness too, and I watched her life fade away with every hacking breath. I tried everything I could to help her get better, researched every known remedy, and tried making some of my own. Nothing worked, and while she was on her deathbed, she made me swear that I'd burn her body, she didn't want me to live with the guilt if I brought her back."

I paused again, feeling the tears gather in my eyes as a lump formed in my throat. "She died, and I burned her like she asked. She was the light of my life, and I felt my will to live burn away with her. When she was nothing except ashes, I locked myself away and felt as empty as the halls were. One day I dropped a jar in the work room, and it cut my finger. The blood dripped onto the floor, and it felt so good. Painful, but the pain was better than the hollowness I felt. I sterilized my sharpest knife and would cut myself as soon as I found myself wishing I was with Imogene or found myself staring at nothing while spiraling down into myself with no escape. " Tears fell.

"How did you stop?" She asked and I heard the sympathy in her voice.

"It was purpose. One day a woman came pounding on my door, screaming that her sister was in labor but was having a difficult time. I helped deliver that baby, and then helped a man with a broken foot, and soon I was so busy that my mind constantly whirled with to-do lists and work that I had no time for pain or the emptiness. I'm scared though." I hadn't voiced this before, but I felt the truth of it ring through me, and it terrified me. "I'm scared that if I don't have enough to do that I'm going to lose myself, like I did last time. I'm scared that if I don't keep moving the ghosts of my past are going to haunt me and pull me under."

It was quiet and I thought that Lys had fallen asleep when she said, "I know I told you about the day I lost this ear," she gestured to the empty spot and I nodded, "but that was also the day I lost one of my closest friends. We're all orphans, in a sense, at the Order, but Dinah was one of the two that I considered my sister. I don't know why I lived when they died, but I made it back to the Order. I didn't want to be alive, though. I felt the guilt wear down on me and was certain that I deserved to be in the ground while they walked and lived. I didn't eat, I was barely human. I don't know how much time passed with me like that, honestly the days and the nights blurred together as if they were a dream and I a sleepwalker. But it was Niamh, the other person I considered a sister, who pulled me out of it. She clutched my hand and when I saw the terror and sleeplessness in her eyes, I knew that I had to live, if only for her. We'd already lost Dinah; she didn't deserve to lose me, too. I get it, Talia, it's human nature to need a reason. When we lose that reason it's easy to drift aimlessly. But we're not alone, Talia, and we can be the reason for each other. I swore to keep you safe, and I'll make another one now. I swear that I'll help you keep moving, and if you feel that lifelessness take over you again, I'll be there to remind you of everything you have to live for."

I laughed. "I'll swear it to you too, Lys. If you ever feel alone or undeserving, I'll be here, reminding you that you could've killed me, but chose to let me live, and that's reason enough for you to live."

She smiled and reached over, two fingers under my chin guiding it up, up, up, and slowly pressed her lips to mine. It was a brief kiss, and the softness of her lips was so at odds with her rough exterior that it caught me off guard. She pulled back and looked at me, giving me time to decide if I wanted to stop. But I didn't and couldn't. I wanted this, and I wanted her. I closed the distance between us, crushing our lips together, my hands going around her waist as she pulled me onto her lap. My legs wound around her hips, and I felt her groan, releasing air into my mouth. Her hands slid between us to cup my butt, the pants I was trying to put on thrown to the side.

"So soft," she sighed into my lips.

With an act of sheer athleticism, she used her position against the bed to stand up, and I clung to her like some deranged monkey. "That's why you work out all of the time," I commented as she laid me down on the bed.

She pressed kisses in quick succession against my collarbone up to my ear. My ear got a sharp nip and my body arched into her, pleasure and pain blurring together. She pulled back and looked at me with an intensity that made me squirm.

"Talia, I…" She looked away briefly, clearly embarrassed. "I want to explore every inch of you, with my eyes, fingers, and tongue. But if you don't want this you need to say something now because I'm not sure I'd be able to stop once I start."

My only response was to pull her mouth back down to mine.

Lys made good on her words, and I felt worshiped. In return, I finally was able to reenact all the dirty things that had been running through my mind these past couple of days. When we were finished showing each other how we felt, we laid panting, our limbs twisted around each other. I was content to never leave again, but I smelled the sweat and grime that clung to me. I trailed soft kisses down the points in her spine before climbing over her and making my way to the bucket of clean-ish water in the bathroom.

"Where are you going?" Lys's voice was muffled by the pillow.

"I've been on the road for almost a week and just sweated due to incredible sex. I'm going to get this grime off me." Feeling bold I continued, "Feel like joining me? I didn't want to ruin the mood, but I'm pretty sure you smell as bad as me."

"So sassy," she said and got off the bed to join me.

We took turns lathering each other up and rinsing ourselves off, lazily exploring the parts we hadn't had a chance to touch yet. I found the mole she has above her hip and she ran a hand over a scar on my knee I got as a kid.

"Have you been with a woman before?" She asked me, and I dropped the soap in surprise.

"No, there was no-one who looked at me like that." I felt a blush coming on.

"How about men?" She asked, clearly intending to make me squirm.

"No, no men either." I did blush then. "What about you?" I asked, eager to get past my embarrassment.

She slowly nodded. "We aren't expected to be celibate, and as long as we were careful the Order didn't care who we spent our time with."

"Women, and men?"

She nodded again. "We grew up knowing that life was valuable, and that everyone's unique and equally important. Love is love; it didn't matter what gender your partner was. I even had some classmates who weren't attracted to anyone, and they were treated the same as everyone else."

"The Order sounds remarkably accepting for something created to eliminate those different from it." I tried to keep the words choked back but they escaped anyways.

"That's why we need you, Talia. To help us be better." She kissed the top of my head, and we finished bathing.

Dried and redressed, we snuggled up against each other in bed, Lys pressing up against my back, her arms slung around me. It was the best sleep I had in my life, and when I would get cold during the night, I was able to turn around and bury myself into Lys's embrace, letting her heat warm my body.

In the morning, we took it slow, neither of us eager to get back to the outdoors. After I re-dosed myself with Philipa's Tincture, we changed and went downstairs, fingertips brushing against each other. Lys brushed a loose strand of hair behind my ear, and I leaned into her affectionately when she smiled down at me. I'd seen a lot of Lys's smiles, but not the easy, bright smile that she wore now. Seeing it made my heart skip a beat.

This was what I'd been missing. Sure, I'd had companionship, Imogene had loved me like her own, and even the townspeople had grown to like and respect me, but I hadn't had someone my age that I could have fun with, or cry with.

"You know, I thought your hair was straight, but it has some curl in it," she pulled on a strand, making it bounce.

"I thought your hair was easy to manage, but this bed head of yours." I clucked teasingly and reached up to ruffle the hair that stuck out at random points.

She smacked my hand away. "How dare you! It's only because I went to bed with it wet."

She tried to flatten it, smoothing it with both hands. When it bounced back to its original position she pouted and laughed. As we entered the main hall she pressed a kiss to my cheek, pulling a sigh out of me.

Her whole body went still at the, "Lysandra?" that came quietly, as if the speaker saw a ghost.

I followed Lys's eyes and saw a woman rise from a table she sat at in the middle of the empty room, a travel pack resting on the floor next to her.

Chapter Thirteen — Lysandra

"It is unknown how mixing Fae blood with human blood resulted in necromancy. What is known is that regardless of how far back in the lineage the Fae parent was, the gene is dominant and will always result in a necromantic offspring. If only Fae blood could have been studied, the applications of it could have been endless."

—Braekios Journal #7, page 12

Oh, no fucking way. I hadn't seen her in over a year, but when she said my name, I knew it was her, Niamh. My eyes flicked to Talia's face, and I almost sighed in relief at the sight of the tinted glasses resting on her nose. In this dreary light, there was no way Niamh would be able to see her eyes. There was a flash of hurt on Talia's face as I took a small step away from her, but I needed to put some distance between us if I was going to think clearly.

"Play along," was all I whispered before going to embrace Niamh, the smile on my face only half-forced.

"Niamh, I can't believe you're here! I've missed you!" Her arms around me were tight and familiar.

"I thought I was seeing things." A large smile lit up her face and I let out a breath I didn't know I held.

Maybe I didn't have to worry too much, after all, while Talia had her glasses on, she didn't look like a necromancer. Plus, the tincture held back the madness. Niamh finally noticed that there was someone else with me and she took Talia in, who stood holding one arm in the other, looking unsure.

"Who's this?" She asked, eying Talia's glasses with a puzzled look while tugging me towards an open seat.

I gestured and Talia approached. "This is Talia, we met up while I was on the road. She's interested in joining the Order and since I was on my way back home, I invited her to travel with me."

It was mostly the truth, Niamh didn't need to know all the details, yet. They shook hands and we ordered breakfast. We spent some time catching up on our friends' whereabouts, and I tried to include Talia in the conversation, but after the fifth soft smile and one-word answer I left her alone to pick at her food silently.

"Where are you coming from, Niamh? The last letter you sent said that you were in the north." We had no address when we were traveling so the best way to get ahold of someone was to send a letter via raven to the Order and hope that it made it, as well as that the recipient was there.

Right before I left for Exela, Niamh had written that she was being sent on a long-term mission in the north and that she'd write to me with her temporary address once she'd gotten there. We wrote back and forth for a bit while I waited to receive my next mission and the last letter I sent was the day before I left for Exela. I guessed she didn't have a chance to receive my letter if she was surprised to see me here, as Noxid was the only town between Exela and Braeton.

Niamh waved her hand dismissively. "I was. I spent almost seven months in the frigid city of Samkiu helping them rebuild after the last attack. I almost didn't believe that it was a group of necromancers that attacked, but there was no way one of them could have done such widespread damage. I was about to head home when I got word of a mission in Norro, so I worked my way down, stopping to track down rogue necromancers. I've never seen so many ghost towns, no people, no ashes, no bodies. It's like they just left. I don't know what's going on, but it feels like they're working towards something."

We were silent and I saw her trying to get past the horrors she had seen. I watched her blink away the past and asked, "What about you, Lys?"

"I was sent down south based on rumors that there was a necromancer hiding out there." I forced my eyes to stay on Niamh's face and not look at Talia as I spoke. "The rumors were right, and I had to fight a necromancer that reanimated the entire town. It was a messy fight, and I lost quite a lot of blood, so I hunkered down in a manor in town until I recovered. Right before I left for the mission though, the Order spoke to us about something called Nectar. Do you know anything about it, Niamh?"

She gulped. "Yes, actually. While I was in Norro, we were attacked, and again it was by a group rather than an individual. They killed all but three of the townspeople and kept drinking from a tiny vial during the fight. I'm assuming that what they drank was Nectar. Once we burned all the bodies, we sent the lab at the Order one of the vials that still had a few drops left and they ran some tests on it. I waited in Norro until I got the results. Turns out the main ingredient is blood. Pure Fae blood. You'd expect there to be some human blood mixed in considering the Fae went extinct, nowadays most necromancers aren't even an eighth Fae, but this blood was one-hundred percent pure Fae. Which is concerning, because that means there's at least one Fae out there that survived the war."

A loud clang had us turning to see Talia picking up the cup she'd been drinking from off the floor. Her face was white and when I knelt to help her, I noticed that her hands trembled.

"What's wrong?" I asked in a low voice, making sure Niamh wouldn't overhear, but I felt her watching us.

Talia only shook her head and said through tight lips, "Not here."

With the water cleaned up, we returned to the conversation, but Talia stayed tense the entire time.

"What I want to know is why they've started working in groups. Do you remember learning about that, because I sure don't," Niamh resumed.

I thought for a moment before responding, "No, you're not wrong. Necromancers are solitary creatures. It's concerning, we're not prepared for that, and I expect there will be way more losses than we're able to handle."

"Great, just what we need," Niamh grumbled before taking a large gulp of something that smelled like beer. "Since you guys are headed to Braeton, do you mind if I tag along? I've been along for so long that I've started talking to the trees around me. I'd love to have someone respond to me."

I nodded, despite wanting to object. I felt Talia begging me to come up with an excuse, but I couldn't say no to this request, not without making Niamh suspicious. Plus, this was Niamh, not only was she a more than capable fighter, but she was my best friend and I'd missed her nearly every day we were apart. I knew her like I knew myself, Niamh was kind and empathetic, there was no way she'd hurt Talia.

"Awesome," Niamh said, standing up after finishing her drink. "I've already paid for my stay, why don't you two go upstairs, pack, and we'll meet down here in, say, three hours? That should give you plenty of time to restock your supplies before we head out."

We agreed and parted ways. The short walk back to our room felt like the longest of my life and I yearned to break the silence that settled between Talia and me. Back inside our room, Talia curled up on the bed, her knees pulled up and her arms cradling her head. I sat down next to her and as I put my arm around her, I felt her shift her weight to lean against me. I tried to rub soothing circles on her legs but the next breath she let out was still unsteady.

"What's going on, Talia? What did Niamh say that has you so spooked?"

"I think it's my father." Her voice was so quiet I wasn't sure I heard her.

"What do you mean?" I knew her father had never been around and that her mother ran away when she was pregnant, but I didn't understand the connection.

She let out another shaky breath. "I think my father's blood is in Nectar. I don't know if he's the one making it, or if someone is using him, but he's a part of all of this."

"Shit, Talia!" I had no idea what to say and tried to find my words. "How can you be sure? This could be a coincidence."

"Think about it, Lys." She raised her head and held my eyes. "We know that Nectar contains blood, and Niamh said that it's pure fae blood. My father was fae. The necromancers who attacked me both said they smelled Nectar in me. The pieces all come together to form one picture. My father's involved with Nectar, and as his assumed only heir, only my blood could be used for Nectar. No other person, necromancer or human, could be used."

I gulped, if this was true, then my promise to keep her safe became a lot more important and harder to keep. "Okay, what does this mean?" We needed a plan, and I had none.

"I don't know. We know that my father escaped the war, it could mean that more survived as well. Which puts everyone in danger."

"If that's true, then we need to get to the Order as soon as possible and warn them. If it's his blood that serves as a power enhancer, do you think yours could be used to nullify its effects?"

She lifted one shoulder. "Maybe? I couldn't say for sure without researching Nectar myself, but it's possible. Which would make my blood valuable to both the Order and him. My anemic future's looking more and more likely once the Order finds out that I'm the only one who can provide insights to the drug."

"Your blood may be important to them, but you're important to me, Talia. You. Your mind, body, and soul. I'm not going to let anyone use you."

I pressed a hard kiss to her forehead, hoping she felt my optimism and confidence. We stayed like that for a few minutes, listening to the noises of the inn around us.

"Should we tell Niamh? About my father?" She asked, rising off the bed.

I let her pull me off the bed. I didn't have to consider my response. "No, we'll tell her when we get to Braeton. If we tell her now, I'm not sure she would hesitate in killing you. I know Niamh, but I've never hid something like this from her, I have no idea how she'll react." This was going to be tricky. "We'll travel together, you'll charm her with your winning personality, and once we're home and less weary, we'll tell her the truth."

"She'd kill me just because of what I am. And yet I'm the monster," Talia said, a hint of her temper putting steel into her eyes.

"You need to understand, Talia, we grew up being taught that our only mission in life was to kill necromancers. Everything we heard and spoke about was the horrors necromancers inflicted on us. We've seen the damage they can do and have lost people close to us, to them. I was ready to kill you until I got to know you. Give her some time. Soon you'll be the best of friends."

"If you say so." I saw the doubt in her eyes.

We packed everything up and journeyed over to the little building advertising it as Noxid's grocer. After paying way too much for low quality vegetables and stale bread, we met up with Niamh in the inn one last time. We handed off our key to Bertilda who accepted it with a grunt and left Noxid.

The walk was pleasant. Sure, the air was cold, the path we walked was winding, but the clouds lacked the tell-tale signs of rain, and I was with the two people I loved the most. Wait… Back the fuck up, what did I say? The *two* people I loved the most? I loved Niamh like family, we'd been together since childhood, but two implied Talia. Did I love her? It hadn't been a month, that was too quick to fall in love, right? I thought about the soft smile she always had while she worked, her determination to move on despite facing constant setbacks and ridicule, her intelligence and empathy, and I knew it was true. I did love her, probably since I saw her first cradle her cat.

I soon found myself lagging behind Niamh and Talia, who discussed plants only found in cold climates, and as my heart settled around this new revelation I stumbled over a rock. They turned around at the sound of my swearing.

"Everything okay?" Talia asked, looking me over.

I hoped she couldn't see the blush on my face, while I knew my feelings wouldn't change, this was not the time to have a life-altering conversation. I tried to make the smile on my face appear natural instead of forced and ran to catch up to them.

Slinging my arms around their shoulders, I may have given Talia's a light squeeze, I steered them back to the road. "All good, tripped over air. You know me!" Niamh raised an eyebrow; she knew something was off. "Talia, do you want to hear the story about how Niamh got caught wearing the Preceptor's robes and almost convinced a merchant that the Order needed a dozen live goats?"

Talia laughed, but Niamh groaned.

"It was a dare! You're not telling it right." She launched into the story, and we spent the rest of the day sharing stories from when we were kids.

Talia even shared one about the unfortunate way she discovered how effective the itching bomb she made was. "I itched for days! Even in spots that weren't exposed to the vapors. My skin was covered in rashes." We laughed with her, and the journey continued. We eventually set up camp, less than a day's walk from Braeton. I could almost see the lights and smell the roasting meat sold in the market square.

I should have known that Talia wouldn't make it to the Order. Should have known that this peace and happiness couldn't last. I wish I could say it went spectacularly wrong. That like a crack of thunder everything fell into disaster, but in reality, it was all due to one small movement.

Talia and Niamh were preparing a fire for dinner when they bumped into each other, causing Talia's glasses to tumble to the ground.

"Sorry about that," Niamh said as she bent down to pick them up.

As she looked up into Talia's stricken face, she hissed, and the glasses fell to the ground again.

"Necromancer." She snarled and lunged for Talia's throat.

Niamh moved fast and I managed to pry Niamh off as Talia had fallen from Niamh's tackle. I pulled her back, putting as much space between us and Talia as the small campsite would allow.

Niamh fought my hold, scratching at my hands and trying to shift her weight to throw me off, all while screaming, "Lys, it's a monster! We need to kill it; you know we need to kill it!"

Just like that, Talia reverted from a person to an it in Niamh's eyes. I was the same way, I realized. When we first met, Talia was nothing but something I needed to kill, but as I got to know her, I saw her humanity. If I could change, so could Niamh.

"Take a breath, Niamh. She's more human than some of the others in the Order. Please, let us explain," I pleaded, hoping I was winning her over.

"It's she, now? How could you let it convince you to let it live? These things killed people, Lys! They killed Dinah, and you're asking me to spare its life? No. If you won't kill it, I will."

She bit my arm, sinking her teeth deep into my flesh, before taking long strides towards Talia. I screamed in pain and in fear for Talia, who finally stood up on shaking legs, looking at us with a dazed expression, and I hoped Niamh didn't give her a concussion from the force of the tackle. I didn't think. I wrestled Niamh to the ground before slamming the hilt of my dagger into the back of her head.

Not sure how long she'd be out, I caught Talia's eye and nodded to a tree. "Help me tie her up. We can make her see reason."

"Are you sure, Lys?" Talia's voice was low, and I could tell she was still wary, but she grabbed Niamh's feet and we slowly brought Niamh to the tree before propping her up and tying her to it.

"Yes, I'm sure, she has to. We'll make her."

I needed Niamh to understand. If we couldn't convince her, we stood no chance in swaying the opinion of the rest of the Order. We sat, watched, and waited for Niamh to wake. Talia's knee bounced and as I put my hand on it to quiet her, I heard her release a deep breath. "I don't know about this, Lys. So much could go wrong. I know you trust her, but I've known people who were cruel for less reasons."

I thought back to when we were children before responding. "She was always the flexible one, Talia. When Dinah and I planned on rubbing poison oak on a classmate's bed because he knocked Dinah out in a match instead of pulling his punch, it was Niamh who told us how he'd been having a lousy day. It was her who told us to give everyone a second chance and to keep an open mind. If I can change my mindset, she can too." I pulled her into my arms, and I felt her relax, just slightly, as my arms enveloped her. "It will be okay, I promise."

Niamh's slumped over form didn't stir until well after the sun had set. I saw the mistrust in her eyes as she looked from Talia to me, and I knew that no matter what happened next, whether she believed us or didn't, our relationship would never be the same.

"Fine," she said after it was clear that we weren't going to say anything. "Tell me."

We did.

Talia told her about her time in Exela, as well as her theory regarding Nectar and her father. I told her about how I found Talia and how we tested Philipa's Tincture. Niamh sat, straight-faced and stony-eyed, through it all, never giving us a sign about how she felt.

Finally, she said "All right, I get it. That's why you two are heading to Braeton. I'll help you, only so that Order can be properly prepared for whatever storm's coming our way. I don't believe it's a coincidence that necromancers have started traveling together and a new drug has sprung up."

I saw Talia relax at this response, and I felt my hands unball from the fists I'd made unconsciously. Treating Niamh so harshly was difficult for me, but I knew it was the right decision. The more people who learned the truth about Talia and still choose to work with us, the better. We could be proof that necromancers and humans couldn't just co- exist together but work together too.

Niamh sighed exasperatedly when she saw that we still hadn't moved from where we sat. "Come on, untie me. It's getting dark and we still haven't eaten yet."

I nodded to a spot out of Niamh's hearing and Talia followed me, Niamh's eyes trailing us as we walked away.

"What do you think?" I asked when we got there. I pulled her in close to me, risking Niamh seeing me to reassure me that Talia's head lacked any tell-tale bumps and that her eyes were able to focus. The last thing we needed was having to stay awake all night to make sure she didn't die in her sleep. Talia let me look her over, but winced slightly when I touched a slightly sensitive spot at the base of her skull.

"I don't know, Lys." She shifted from one foot to the other. "She's your friend, but she was so quick to attack. How about this? We knock her unconscious so that she couldn't shout for help. It'd give us a head start and let us get to the Preceptor before she does. Someone will eventually come along and untie her. Or she'll do it herself, you did escape your ropes, after all."

"You want to leave her here? Tied up, where anyone and anything can attack her? Come on, Talia, you're smarter than that. There's a better way to do this, I need to think for a minute."

"I didn't say it was a good idea, but I can't think of anything else. I did take a nasty fall." Talia sulked and I tried to think of a way to convince both her and Niamh that we could still travel together.

"She would be a powerful ally and we could use all that we can get. You trust me, and I trust her. If she says that she's going to help us, she will." I took her hands, running my thumb over her knuckles. She looked at me and the starlight of her eyes had me kissing her tenderly, her lips warming mine in the cold air.

I didn't care that Niamh watched, I needed to reassure Talia that I wouldn't let anything, or anyone harm her.

She sighed and kicked a rock towards Niamh. "Fine. If you believe her, then that'll have to be good enough for me."

We walked back to Niamh, hand in hand, and I saw Niamh's eyes narrow in anger and betrayal, but all she said was, "Untie me. My butt's starting to hurt and since nothing I've said got through to you, I'll help. You're clearly enamored, Lys. When it, I mean Talia, inevitably breaks your heart, I'll be there to pick up the pieces, like I always have. Have you forgotten how poorly all your past relationships have turned out? I can't imagine one with a necromancer going any better."

With all of that out of the way, we ate dinner. Providing a peace offering, Niamh even shared some wine she brought with her from Samkiu, which was known for a secretive recipe that helped cultivate grapes year-round. I could tell she was still unhappy and mistrustful, but she didn't say anything nasty to Talia, even calling her by name, so I figured that everything was okay. My head felt fuzzy, no doubt from the wine, and I found myself nodding off, so I excused myself and fell into a deep dreamless sleep.

"Lys! Lysandra!" Talia's panicked and desperate screams woke me, and when my hand didn't find her in her normal spot next to me, I scrambled to find her.

Talia was tied up against the same tree we had Niamh against mere hours ago. It felt like it had been only a few hours since we had dinner, but the sun was deep into the sky. Niamh crouched down in front of Talia, one hand holding a knife to Talia's throat, the other holding Talia's face in a cruel grip. She stared into Talia's eyes, unflinching, occasionally turning it side to side, as if she looked for something. I hoped she searched for the madness, and that once she didn't find it, she'd release Talia.

"Lysandra! Please! Help!" The terror in her eyes, the warble in her voice drove me to my feet, only to stumble and fall to the ground.

I looked down at the ropes binding my feet and hands together in confusion. Talia must've seen that I wouldn't be able to free her because she stopped screaming and closed her eyes.

"Niamh, what are you doing? You said that you'd help us. I trusted you!" The words were pulled from deep within me, and I felt my throat constrict on them.

The response I got from Niamh ripped my soul in two. "I trusted you, Lysandra. I trusted you to know that it's us against them. Trusted that you wouldn't be naive enough to fall for some pretty thing that showed you an ounce of attention. Trusted you to not choose this monster over me, the person who stayed by your side as you wasted away and waited for you to realize everything you have to live for. Did Dinah's death mean nothing to you?"

I saw nothing of the Niamh I knew in the eyes that looked back at me. There was no warmth or empathy that I grew up around. I knew that our time in the Order changed us, but I couldn't believe that this was the person it shaped Niamh into, cruel and merciless.

She trailed the dagger down Talia's neck to her forearm. "It's fitting, I think, that I do this with Dinah's dagger."

It was then that I saw the familiar hilt, the blade I grew to know so well, dig into Talia's flesh. Talia let out a scream so shrill and pained, birds took flight from the sound. Niamh took her time, slicing slowly from Talia's left elbow to her wrist, before switching to the right and doing it all over again. "Consider this a mercy, necromancer. You'll take longer to bleed out than if I slit your throat. Take this time to watch your lover choose to walk away from you."

"No!" I screamed, and crawled my way across the floor, the tears soaking the dirt in front of me. My fingernails broke on the hard ground, and I felt my pants rip thanks to a rock, but I couldn't let it slow me down. I had to do something, anything, but I was powerless. Talia's eyes rolled back into her head, and her head fell forward, the blood soaking the ground. I knew there was nothing I could do, nothing except weep for the person who held my heart in her hands.

"Look at that. It bleeds red after all." Niamh stood, brushed the dirt off her pants, hoisted up her backpack, and grabbed my hands. She wrenched me up. "Walk. The monster will die here, but you don't need to. We're going back home, and you're going to tell them everything. We're going to continue, killing every fucking necromancer around. You'll become the poster child for why we can't trust necromancers, and why they deserve the deaths we give them. Do you understand?"

My feet dragged under me, my vision was gray and growing darker, as my heart cracked with each second. "We needed her! We needed her skills, her brain. Why, Niamh?" I would never be able to separate Niamh from this moment, would never be able to see her face and not feel the ground beneath my feet disappear.

"Why? Because I have the tincture she made. If some country bumpkin can make it, then so can the Order. More importantly, you need to be reminded of whose side you're on and where your priorities should align."

"I've always done what's best for the Order. I lived for the Order, and I will die for the Order. Talia was the only thing I had for myself, and even she agreed to help the Order. She could have made us better!"

I had nothing left to say, already saw myself fade away back to the nothingness I was when Dinah died, with no intention of emerging from it this time around. I let Niamh drag me behind her, refusing to help her return me to the place that would be forever haunted by what could've been. My eyes never strayed from Talia's body, and with every inch I was dragged away from her, I knew that I'd died with her. We were almost out of eyesight when I saw something. It might have been a trick of the light, or her body reacting postmortem, but I swear I saw her left-hand twitch. Hope filled me and I almost ran to her. But if I did, Talia would be in danger again. I begged the universe to keep her alive and reunite us, but knew that even if it was possible, it would be a long while before I saw her again. I couldn't leave her without knowing that I spoke the words aloud, even if it was to her cooling corpse.

"You know, Niamh, it isn't just that the Order needed her. I needed her. I needed her smile to make me feel alive, her laugh to remind me it was okay to enjoy the day."

"I don't care," was all I got, and I was yanked harshly.

I continued, raising my voice, hoping that Talia could hear me. "It's not even that I needed her. I loved her. I loved her with every breath in my body and every thought in my head. I will always love her and there will never be another."

I began to plot, determined to find my way back to her. She might be dead, lost to me forever, but if there was even a slight chance that she was alive, I'd have to take it. I'd let Niamh drag me back to the Order, convince everyone I was back to being the perfect chasseur full of remorse and eager to begin anew, and then I'd reunite with Talia, in whatever way I could. There would be no returning after that, I'd be exiled from the Order and wouldn't dare to show my face in Braeton, but it didn't matter. I'd find Talia, with her I could see a future of peace, and I'd kill anyone and anything for that.

Chapter Fourteen — Talia

"Necromancers are solitary creatures, two or more cannot exist in the same space without death. It is unknown why they are incapable of living in groups, though there is speculation that it is due to the lack of resources that forces conflict."

—Braekios Journal #2, page 7

I drifted. My mind wandered between dream and nightmare, and I couldn't make sense of anything. Lys screamed that she loved me as she was dragged away from me, only for me to be the one bound, the love in Lys's eyes turned into hatred as she lit a fire beneath me. I tried to run but was frozen, forced to watch the flames slowly climb up my legs.

"You honestly thought I could love something like you? What a pathetic little monster." Her voice was devoid of any emotion except disgust.

She stood there, watching as I screamed and writhed as the flames climbed higher, covering my mouth, my nose, creeping around my eyes. But before I saw nothing but the fire, I found myself back in my room in Exela, listening to the voices on the other side of the door.

"She's getting worse, can't this damn thing go any faster?!"

What an odd thing to say, I felt fine. I tried to tell the high pitch voice clipped with panic this, but found my mouth full of gravel.

"I'll tell you again, no. This is a long trip, if we go any faster, we're going to kill the horses before we get there. Plus, you already gave her Nectar, there's nothing else we can do." This voice was deep and clearly not as concerned. Weird, if this was a dream I should recognize those voices as belonging to the townspeople, but I didn't.

"If she dies before we get there, we'll be the ones killed." This came from the higher voice, angry instead of panicked. "Pick up the pace!"

It made no sense, I was in my room, I wasn't going anywhere. The cold walls pressed in on me. I grabbed the doorknob and twisted it, but it didn't move. I called out for help and scratched at the door, hoping to claw my way out, but I was incapable of doing anything except splitting open my fingertips. Pressing a blood-tinged finger to my mouth, I sucked on it, hoping to stop the bleeding. The blood tasted wrong and when I pulled it back out of my mouth, I saw that it was black instead of red. I knew that it wasn't human.

I screamed and the voice on the other side of the door said, "Shit! She's opening her wounds quicker than they can heal! Quick, give me the syringe, I'm putting her back under."

I felt a sharp prick in my arm and nothing more. My nightmares turned into never-ending static, and I let myself fall into it.

I finally woke up and found myself not in Exela or the campsite I last remembered, but in an unfamiliar room. I was on a stiff bed with a light white sheet to keep me warm. The walls were bare except for a single window curtained by white gauze which swayed in the warm breeze. Where was I? The nights were getting colder as I was traveling with Lys, there was no way I slept until spring. My heart sputtered to a halt. Lys, where was she? What happened? The memories rushed back, the tree, Lys tied up on the ground sobbing, the dagger… My eyes darted to my arms, and I saw thick white bandages wrapped around them slightly stained red from my blood. I picked up my left arm to look closer and hissed in pain.

"They got you good, whoever did that. It's a miracle you're still alive." That voice, I knew it, not from my dreams, but from sometime before then.

Leaning against the doorframe was the necromancer from the woods with the striking violet eyes. I took in more of her now that it was light out and I was able to see more of her features. Her skin was dark and luminous, the contrast of it to her eyes making her even more alluring. Her hair fell over her shoulders to her waist in thick black rivulets held back with little gold bands. She was gorgeous, and judging by the smirk she gave me, she knew it. She wore tight black pants and a tan wool sweater rolled up to her elbows. I looked back down to myself and saw that I wore identical clothes.

"Your clothes were a mess and we're the closest in size, so I loaned some of them to you. I expect them to be washed before I get them back, I don't want any of that filthy human smell clinging to you to transfer." She came into the room and sat on a stool next to me, resting an elbow on the small nightstand next to the bed, almost knocking off the glass of water that sat there. "Why you choose to live with them for so long is a mystery to me. The only good human is a dead human." She practically spat the words out and I found myself flinching away from the venom in her words despite not considering myself human for quite some time.

"Look," My voice came out raspy and I swallowed to clear the dust in my mouth before trying again, "I don't know who you are." I raised my eyebrows since she clearly forgot to introduce herself. "But I don't appreciate you coming in here and insulting my choices. Why don't you run along and tell whoever is in charge that I'm awake and pissed off."

"Touchy touchy," she said, rising to walk back to the door, hopefully to follow my instructions and inform her superior that I was awake. "The name's Rae, by the way," she threw my way before leaving me.

I sighed, glad that I had a moment of peace to process my sudden change in company and location. I hoped that Lys was okay. Niamh seemed confident that Lys could be rehabilitated, but

I had the feeling that if Lys couldn't be, she'd find herself betrayed again and bleeding out. I felt flushed and my body warmed with anger at how we'd both been treated.

Damn it! I finally had something good, I was finally going to do something meaningful with my abilities. The tears fell, hot and thick, a reminder that there was always something or someone you could lose. I heard footsteps approaching and wiped them away, refusing to let whoever was coming see my weakness. I took deep breath after deep breath, trying to calm down when he finally arrived.

"Talia," he said, low and full of a familiarity he shouldn't have. "I've been looking for you."

"Hello, Father." For there was no one else this could be. He matched the bits and pieces of description that I'd dragged out of my mom over the years, a straight nose, full lips that seemed to smile with kindness instead of the cruelty they spread, blond wind-swept hair the same color as mine. The only difference between what I was told and what I saw was the red eyes that narrowed at me now. He found a way to reverse the magic he used to change his eye color, and I peered at his ears to see if the tips had returned as well. When he noticed where my gaze fell his smile turned into a sneer. His aura exuded control. I felt it slowly creep around me, stifling the breeze that entered the room and trying its best to force me into submission.

"Good, you know who I am. When your traitor of a mother ran off and hid you, I worried that you wouldn't know your heritage. I was concerned that you'd take after her, but I see that my blood flows strongly through you."

His hand reached out to tuck a loose strand of hair behind my ear and I suppressed a shudder.

"Tell me, child." His hand went to my throat, rubbing over the pulse there. "Why would you help humans when you know that we fought and lost against their kind in the past? They think they own this land, when it's ours. It belongs to us, who still feel the call of it, not to the ones who turned away from it when the land was in desperate need of protection." I longed to argue with him, to remind him that necromancers were part human, we didn't participate in that war long ago, and that our abilities fed off death, not life. But I couldn't. His hand tightened on my bruised throat, cutting off my airway and any thought I had of responding.

I grabbed at his hands, trying to pry them off.

"Luther told me about your claim to have something that could counter necromantic abilities," he continued, uncaring that he was on his way to killing his only child.

The room grew fuzzy.

"Rae saw you with a human and I knew that you turned traitor, too. Like your whore of a mother. She may have tried to hide you, but I found you again. Let me tell you what I didn't have the chance to tell your mother. You are mine, from the breath you take to the thoughts you form in your head. As my daughter, there are certain expectations I have for you. Expectations that you've failed to meet in the past. That will cost you, unfortunately."

All I saw was a tunnel, the only light, the red in his eyes.

"But I am a kind and just father. I'll let you off with a warning."

He sounded far away, and his red eyes drowned me as my hands fell to my side.

"You will obey me. Or I will kill anything you value and make you reanimate it, so you will be reminded of the choice you made."

I felt nothing, not his hand leaving my throat, nor my head hitting the pillow, I was surrounded by the fuzzy darkness I'd just woken from.

When I awoke again, Rae was back on the stool, a new glass of water on the side table next to her. I pushed myself up into a seated position and when I opened my mouth, she pushed the cup into my hands.

"Don't try to speak. The General severely damaged your throat, if you try to talk now, you'll make it worse."

Rae saw me looking for a way to ask a question and she handed me a notebook and pen.

"The General?" I wrote, my handwriting a little shaky. I hoped that Lys was having a better time than I was, this was the second near death experience I'd had in about as many weeks.

She leaned over and read what I wrote before responding. "Yeah, General Ostyx. He's in charge of everyone here."

Great, that didn't answer very much.

At the "Here?" I wrote in capital letters, Rae looked confused. "Did he not explain anything to you?" I shook my head and she sighed. "He doesn't have the best people skills." My hand gravitated to my neck, and I shot her a look. "I know, he was harsh on you. But you're his daughter, he has to be. He's not like that with the rest of us." I continued to stare at her, hoping she'd explain what was going on. She slapped her knees and stood up. "All right, let the tour begin!"

She ripped the blanket off me, and I shivered slightly before swinging my legs over the bed and stood on unsteady feet, eager to learn more about where I found myself. Rae pulled me towards the door, all I could do was stumble after her. The hallway we exited into was stone, with large windows every few feet. I stopped and could do nothing except stare. We must've been at the top of a hill because I looked out over a small town, the roofs all terracotta brown and slightly faded from the sun, but none needing repair. Past the town was a row of trees, deep green and tall, and beyond them, the ocean, pure blue and reaching towards the horizon.

Rae let me take it all in before coming over to the window and taking in the view herself.

"Welcome to Syrenthia," she breathed.

"Where are we?" I wrote as I took in the salty breeze and the sun beating down on me. I pushed up my sleeves, finally warm.

"Only those who need to travel to the mainland know the exact location, but what I can tell you is it's a small island that was once a refuge for the Fae who managed to escape the war. There were more than we were led to believe. Many, like your dad, saw the war ending in the human's favor and slipped away in the night. They lived here for centuries, never leaving, isolated and trying to start over. In the end, it was the isolation that killed them. When a large hurricane came, it wiped out all the island's residents. When they died, it went unused, until General Ostyx invited us here."

"How did he know it was here if everyone died?" The words were smeared across the page in my haste to ask the question before she continued.

Rae leaned over to read my question. "He had friends here that he'd come to visit. He lived nearby with his family, and when the Fae needed something they couldn't get here, they'd sail across and give him a list of necessities. The way he tells it, the day of the hurricane he was tied up and couldn't reach them in time."

I gulped and wondered if the day of the hurricane was the same day my mom finally escaped.

Rae continued, not noticing the way I grew still. "When he was able to get to Syrenthia again, all his friends were dead. He rebuilt the place, moving the main town further inland, and once he was done, he ventured back out and began to find necromancers in need of a home. Come on, I'll show you around."

We walked through the hall and down the stairs as Rae explained that the building we were in served as the town hall, and Ostyx's residence when he wasn't on the mainland. "You were asleep for longer than we anticipated, so we were able to finish cleaning your home. The previous resident died, and it got a bit dusty."

Outside, I looked up at the giant stone building behind us, taking in the history that it must've seen as the only original structure that survived the hurricane. We walked down a large stone staircase, past trees lush with fruit, green grass, and plenty of flowers, into the town. I saw necromancers everywhere, eyes in shades of orange, green, purple, and blue, walking together, smiling and laughing. There were vendors giving away aromatic breads that had my stomach reminding me that I hadn't eaten in a long time. We stopped to get some of the bread and Rae chatted with the vendor who shot me nervous looks when he thought I wasn't looking. I used the break to look closer at my surroundings. Tall palm trees stood at attention on either side of the road, providing shade where little children played in the grass, taking turns to roll a little ball close to a target. The other vendors sold things ranging from clay plates and pots to little wooden toys, set up shop under tan awnings in front of the homes. I saw an older woman, her hair gray and wiry, stick her head out of the window to shout at a man selling cool milk. At her gesture, he brought over a jug of it and handed it through the window. The woman disappeared, and I saw no money exchanged. I wondered how people paid for goods here but had my answer when the woman returned with some soap. I guessed that being away from the mainland meant they had no use for money, choosing to use a bartering system instead.

With a nudge from Rae the vendor, a man with skin the color of freshly polished wood, addressed me directly. "I hope that you like it here, Miss. Rae tells me that you're an accomplished herbalist. That's something we've been missing for a very long time. If you ever need any help, please don't hesitate to ask. I'll make sure you always have something warm to eat." I nodded, uncomfortable, and Rae thanked the vendor before continuing with the tour.

"How many necromancers are here?" This place almost didn't seem real, but everyone here was relaxed, and I couldn't see a single human.

She thought for a minute. "Around two hundred, I think? Though most of those are under the age of twenty or over the age fifty."

My hand scribbled across the page, so many more questions crowding my brain. "How did you get here? Why are you all here?"

"I'll answer everything I can, but there are some things I can't tell you. Ostyx found me when I was little, I think around five, though I don't know my birthday so I could be off by a few years. I was on the brink of death. No family, no one to care if I lived or died, except for him. He picked me up and brought me here. He found others who were living on the outskirts of life and needed help. He's been bringing more and more here, and we've made this place into a home again. We're here because we were tired of being hunted and killed simply because of what we are. But that's going to change."

What did she mean by change? She saw my questioning look but refused to answer. "Never mind that for now. Ostyx will tell you himself when he has time. Come on, I want to show you something."

We continued walking and I took in the necromancers we passed by from lowered eyes, trying not to look as if I stared. I received many skeptical looks, and children were ushered into houses only to peer at me from windows outside of their guardians' eyes. Rae brought me to a small house with a bedroom, a kitchen, bathroom (with indoor plumbing, much to my delight), and a work room. It was all so like Exela that my heart skipped a beat.

"We know that you were an herbalist in your past life. Like Mikel said, we don't have anyone with that kind of expertise here and a lot of people get sick this time of year. I know you didn't come here willingly, and you probably resent us for it, but this could be your home, too. You're one of us, I know you'll fit right in. Please, won't you stay?"

She had a hopeful smile, but her eyes were desperate. This place felt like home, and that concerned and confused me. What was it about here that made me think of Exela? It might've been the way the ocean waves sounded so like the way the wind traveled across the lake back in Exela, or the way that despite the world telling them that they were better off alone, they chose to live together in harmony, but something told me to say yes and stay here. Lys may have made it back to Braeton, but I had no clue where I was or how to get back to her.

I looked around, taking inventory of what I would need to stock up on and wrote, "Tell me where to start."

My days fell into an easy and familiar routine. I'd wake up and get breakfast from one of the vendors before beginning my work for the day. I made poultices to help with scraped knees and cuts, distributing them as people came in. I set noses broken during rough play or when someone took a fall down the many stairs leading up to the main estate. I'd make house-visits to sick families and deliver babies. Rae came and visited often, helping me grind up plants or setting stuff away. She spoke to me of her time running around the island and growing up away from humans, and I told her about my time in Exela. I could tell she didn't enjoy hearing about my time helping humans, but she was willing to listen. In the evenings, I'd go down to the ocean and listen to the waves, imaging Lys swimming among them or running up and down the beach. I didn't know what she was doing, but I hoped she was well.

I always kept an eye trained on the horizon, hoping that I'd eventually spot someone coming or going to the mainland. I never stopped trying to find a way back to Lys. There were no boats bobbing near the beach, and when I asked Rae how they got to the mainland, she shrugged and told me not to worry about it. I didn't know if I'd ever get back to Lys, and every morning I woke up without her, I fought back the feeling of loss. The weeks passed and I thought of her every day, what our life could've been like, and if she loved me the way I loved her.

My door opened one day, and I turned to the unwanted visitor, my father.

"I came to see how you were settling in," he said, walking around and examining the jars and dried plants I had around the main room that I used as a clinic. I had a back room with two cots for when a patient needed to stay overnight, but those were currently empty. I doubted seeing my clinic was the only reason he was here.

"How can I help you?" I asked, with a sticky sweet voice I used for those I disliked the most.

He smiled and opened the door, gesturing for me to follow. "Fancy a field trip?"

Knowing that he'd drag me out if I refused, I followed, being sure to place a "be back soon" sign on the front door. We walked up the stairs to the manor, and past the room I first woke up in. At a large brown door, my father pulled out a large key. The key must've been iron because he hissed at the contact, and he quickly returned the key to a thick cloth bag before ushering me down a large dimly lit staircase.

One more door, but this one wasn't locked, and we lit a torch inside as my eyes adjusted to the darkness. When I could finally see I had to gulp down the terror I felt. I was pushed forward, and he walked behind me, past locked cells full of filthy humans who cowered back from us, eyes haunted.

"Humans have lived long enough," my father began, running his fingers along the bars. "It's taken me centuries of experiments and research, but I've finally figured it out." He paused, clearly expecting me to respond. When I didn't, he continued. "The Fae were too dependent on the land and expected the humans to fight with honor. That was their downfall. But these necromancers—they know that humans are trash and are willing to do what must be done. War's coming, and you'll be leading it, by my side."

Here I finally did respond. "What's with these humans, then?"

"We'll need an army when the time's right. Who could defeat an army that would fight without feeling the sting of steel cutting into them? Humans are only good for one purpose, serving as our weapons. Humans may be able to defeat one necromancer and the handful of corpses they control, but they will cower before the coordinated force I've been building. With Nectar, my necromancers will be even stronger, able to control more dead for longer."

"What is Nectar?" I asked as nonchalantly as I could.

"It's an accelerant, a concoction that contains pure Fae blood. My blood," he said with a smile, "is connected to the land. By mixing it with some of the plants unique to Syrenthia, a necromancer can tap into the land's raw power and use it. It also speeds up their healing abilities. It's thanks to Nectar that you healed as fast as you did. Though, there are some backlashes from Nectar. Humans, even part humans, aren't meant to channel Fae capabilities. Using Nectar for an extended time can greatly reduce a necromancer's life span. But frequent use is necessary, they can't stop using it once they begin or they'll die from withdrawal."

"Why distribute it, Dad? Why send necromancers from Syrenthia to distribute it if you know it's driving them to an early death if they can't get more?"

"They're all dispensable. The necromancers on the mainland serve as my war hounds. They'll cull the weak before my forces come in and exterminate the rest."

"Your work hasn't gone unnoticed. The Order kept track of every necromancer who mentioned Nectar and they've been trying to figure out the source."

He laughed. "Let them come. I don't fear the Order. Now, Talia, are you with us, or will you sit by and watch as I kill all that you love?"

I had to stop him, that much I knew, but I couldn't do it right now, not by myself. "I'm with you, General," I said before bowing my head slightly, a subordinate showing respect to its leader. He smiled one more time before escorting me home, past the blank eyes that stared at us beyond the cell bars.

I had a responsibility, now that I knew Ostyx's plan, to the humans who cowered in the cells below this island as well as to the ones who lived on the mainland. I couldn't let Ostyx start another war, we had only just begun to forget the effects of the last one. There had to be a way I could send a message to Lys and the Order, preparing them for what was to come. Syrenthia held a small population, sure, but it needed the occasional supply that could only be imported from the mainland, mainly materials used in repairing the buildings. The trips to gather the materials weren't made frequently and I had no idea when the next trip was, so I prepared myself for a long wait. I began to be expected in the town square around noon, with a book in hand, to take in the sunlight. I paid little attention to my book though, and chose to listen and watch what happened around me, hoping I'd hear snatches of conversation talking about the exciting idea of a new haul from the mainland that may include the occasional treat, like silk or some other processed textile the islanders couldn't get from their livestock. It took a few days, but soon I saw the grocer walking around to all the residents with a small notebook. When she was done talking to the couple who lived next to me, I placed myself in her way.

Her eyes widened in slight alarm, but she smiled at me. "You're the new herbalist, aren't you? How can I help you?"

I gestured to where my clinic was down the street. "I heard rumors that you're gathering requests for the next trip to the mainland." She gulped and I knew that I guessed right. "I was hoping to request a few herbs. With the wet season coming, they'll be crucial in keeping us all healthy. Unfortunately, I haven't been able to find any here." She followed me down the street and into my clinic. The door clicked behind us, and I guided her to a nearby chair.

"If you can give me a list, I'm sure I could try to acquire a few," she said, resting an arm on the table next to her.

"Thank you! I wrote down a list, somewhere…" I rummaged around in the desk I used for my documents, hoping she didn't see the small knife I pulled out from a drawer. She watched me for a few seconds before growing disinterested and looked through the window at the people walking by.

I walked up behind her and pressed my knife against her neck, making the jewelry she wore there tinkle. "I need you to get a message to a friend of mine, Lysandra Spits, in Braeton." I hoped she made it there okay. I wasn't sure if Niamh killed her after she tried to kill me.

The grocer started to shake her head, but when my knife pricked against her throat, she stopped. "That's where the Order resides, why would I go there?"

"I'm Ostyx's daughter." Her eyes widened. I guessed that wasn't public knowledge. Oh well, if Ostyx didn't want people knowing he had a child, he shouldn't have brought me here.

"His blood runs through me. If you can deliver this message, I'll give you a month's supply of Nectar."

"Deal!" She said quickly, and I knew she was addicted to the stuff. "I know where Braeton is, it shouldn't take me too long to get there!"

"Not so quick," I said, leaning down to whisper in her ear. "If you come back, and I find out you didn't do as I asked, I will kill you and force you to do my bidding."

She agreed again and I let her loose to write a quick message, explaining where I was and what I knew before asking for aid. The small group traveling to the mainland was scheduled to leave two days from now, and would take around three days to reach the mainland, depending on how choppy the sea was. There was nothing else I could do, except wait, and hope that my message reached the Order. The team that left for the mainland returned a week later, except the grocer. She was last spotted separating from the group after saying she was going to visit a nearby farm for some specialty produce and never returned. The team waited the designated two days before writing her off as killed and returned home. The night I learned of her assumed demise, I couldn't sleep. I had no way of knowing if my message reached Lys or if I would have any help. After picking up my blanket that had fallen off me for the fifth time that night, I decided to put my plan into action. If I couldn't count on any help, I would have to do it all myself, starting with getting the captive humans out of here. I needed food, water, and clothing that would protect us from the sun as we traveled over the ocean. None of this would mean anything, though, if I couldn't find the boats they kept secret.

That night I prowled around the island searching for them, going as far as scaling a short cliff to get to a small sandy beach that was barely visible. When I was above the beach, I let go of the rocky wall with the intent of landing agilely on my feet. Instead, I fell on my ass with a loud *oomph*. The bruise on my butt would be worth it though, because when I turned around, I saw a glorious sight—boats! Three mid-sized boats bobbed peacefully in the water, which was two more than I'd hoped for. Ostyx clearly learned from the demise of the Fae and prepared a way for the islanders to evacuate if needed and for the first time in my life, I approved of something my father did. I waded out into the warm water and saw no locks, just ropes keeping them tethered. After double checking that all the boats were intact, I climbed up again, looking for an easier way to get to the beach. As the sun slowly rose, I saw a small path I originally overlooked and used it to run home. I managed to make it home in time for a visit from Rae. I quickly gathered breakfast and as we ate, I tried to think of something to talk about, only to find my brain solely occupied by my escape plan, and we finished the meal in silence. She stayed around for a while, helping me restock my salves and potions. Everything about the day was normal, and yet I couldn't help feeling on edge. Rae reached over to take a jar from me, and I flinched back from her, the jar slipping from my fingers. The jar shattered against the ground, and I bent down to clean it up, trying to come up with a believable lie to explain my jumpiness.

"That jar contains some ingredients that cause a rather awful rash before being mixed with others. I applied a balm to my hands so I could handle it safely, but I forgot to tell you to put some on. You didn't get any on your skin, did you?"

She shook her head, but I saw her trying to figure out if she believed my story.

We walked around the town handing out the latest batch of bug repellent and I ran over the plan in my head. I had enough of a wardrobe to make hats and other sun protection for a couple dozen humans, and I could easily buy food and bottled water from the vendors once Rae left. I couldn't get a good look at the humans with my father, and while I hoped I could get them all out, I feared I'd have to be selective. I was caught up in my thoughts and I could tell that Rae knew that something was on my mind, putting herself in my path to get my attention.

"Want to meet up for dinner? We can drink and talk shit about your nosy neighbors."

I couldn't refuse the invite, so she came over and we had a tense night despite the liquor that flowed.

When Rae left late into the night, I knew I didn't have long to put my plan into action. I feared that she'd tell my father that I acted suspiciously, and if he strangled me for the choices I made in the past, I worried what he'd do to me if he found out. I laid in bed, staring at the ceiling for a few hours, making sure that Rae wasn't lurking around somewhere watching me, and grabbed my darkest cloak and slipped onto the road. I hurried through the trees and chose to take a steep path up to the manor instead of the main stairs. Once again in front of the large wooden door, I fished out the metal tweezers I used to extract wood splinters from a lumberjack earlier that week. I shoved them inside and wiggled them around, fearing discovery as the seconds ticked past. There was a loud click, and I pulled open the door. I closed it behind me, plunging me back into darkness, and I carefully ran down the steps into the depth of the basement. I paused at the bottom door to light a torch.

The sight of rows of cells full of human prisoners had me falling to my knees. There were easily a couple hundred down here, way more than I'd first seen, and the stench that wafted towards me as well as the haunted look in their eyes told me they'd been down here for a while. Niamh had mentioned ghost towns, guess I found their residents. I brought over the lantern to the closest cell, raising it to get a better look at the humans in it. They shrank back from the light, and I saw mothers pull their children behind them, trying to protect them.

"It's okay. I'm here to help. Can you tell me how many there are of you?" They were silent and I tried again. "Please, I really am here to help, I'm with the Order and I'm going to get you back to your homes. But I need to know how many people are down here."

A young man with shaggy black hair and a long beard limped forward and I saw that he was missing a foot. "I saw you with the Fae General, necromancer. You can't be with the Order." His voice was low and scratchy from the lack of use.

"I'm a necromancer, but I'm not like the ones here. My friend, Lys, convinced me to join the Order. We were on our way there before I was attacked and brought here." She was so much more than a friend, but they didn't need to know that.

"Do you mean Lysandra? Lysandra Spits?" His voice had a hint of awe to it.

"Yes?" I asked, uncertain as to how he knew the name.

"My name's Lucien. I grew up with Lysandra. If she trusts you, I'll trust you. We can trust her!" He said, throwing his voice to the back of the cell on the last sentence, and I saw a ripple of excitement travel through the group.

"Lucien, I have a plan, but I need to know how many there are of you."

"It's hard to know. There were originally around five hundred of us, but many of us have died. I'm not sure that those of us that are still alive would be able to walk out of here, food and water have been sparse and irregular."

There were that many of them? Even if there were only a fifth of what he told me, that was too many to fit on the few boats I did see at the beach.

"Okay," I swallowed, trying to come up with a new plan. "I need to rethink this. I didn't expect so many of you. But I promise I'll get you out."

"I doubt that." I whirled around at the harsh chuckle that accompanied that statement, to see my father leaning against the door, several men behind him.

"My dear Talia, I wish you wouldn't continuously disappoint me. Rae has been telling me about the good work you've done for us, but when she told me that you were acting strange tonight, I had a feeling that something was going on. Get her."

The men ran towards me and pulled me from the bars, Lucien shrinking back. They dragged me deeper into the basement, past dozens of cells all occupied, and I saw large shallow eyes staring at me, not in fear, but in pity. Because they knew what it was like down here. I was thrown into the last cell, and I fell to the damp straw as the door was closed and locked. Water dripped down the walls slowly, and I scrambled to find any source of light to drive away the darkness.

"No, Father, please don't do this! You know this is wrong!"

"Is it?" He asked, looking at me through the bars. "They wiped us out, it's only fair that we repay the favor. You'll remain here until they're all dead. But don't worry, my darling, I won't kill you, your blood will serve a purpose. For now, though, you'll stay here, and wonder at what's happening. I hope your thoughts contain nothing but fear for your precious humans. Maybe when I see you next, you'll be a little more open minded."

He left, taking the light with him, and I sank into the darkness, fearing what was going to come.

I was woken up with a slap to my face and opened my eyes to see my father standing above me.

"Good morning, Talia. Have you decided to join us?"

I brought my hand to my stinging cheek and swallowed, knowing that he wouldn't like the answer. "No, Father. I won't help you."

He sighed and jerked his head towards me. I scrambled back against the wall as two of the men from the previous night stalked towards me.

Shackles were put on my hands and feet, and I was dragged up two flights of stairs and thrown into a work room like my own, except for the cruel-looking instruments reflecting the light from the lantern. I screamed and fought but was shackled to a table in the middle of the room.

"I hoped that you'd understand, Talia. But you made your choice, and it was the wrong one. You may not fight by my side, but you can still be of use. You're only half Fae, so the drug won't be as potent, but I can still use your blood to make Nectar. It'll be nice not to have to cut myself constantly."

He placed a knife to my arm, sitting it right against the new scar that began at my elbow, still not fully healed from Niamh's slicing. "This'll hurt you, Talia, but know that you'll help many more." With that, he pressed down, and fire erupted in my veins as the knife cut me open.

Chapter Fifteen — Lysandra

"Through multiple interviews done at the end of their lives, I have learned that none regret their actions, or wished to be human. Their pride and arrogance ensure that humans and necromancers will never be able to coexist."

—Braekios journal #8, page 34

I was being watched. All the fucking time. Every time I went to sleep there was someone sitting in the corner, every time I walked down the hall someone was three steps behind me, every time I went to cook, as soon as my hand reached for the knife, it was taken from me. It was exhausting and I was on edge every day, but I plastered a fake smile on my face, determined to make the Order trust me again.

The first two weeks back were difficult. I had to repent. Which meant I was kept isolated and locked in one of the cells in the basement, only visited when it was time for me to list my multitude of wrongs and how my actions caused harm to the Order. Again and again, I was reminded of our cruelty towards necromancers. Again and again, I decided to hold us accountable and do better. There were no windows and the days blurred together, separated only by the time I was given meals. When they felt I had been properly starved and remorseful, I was brought out into the nearby towns desecrated by necromancer attacks. I watched as the bodies burned and was forced to interview the survivors, asking them to relive their worst moments, all under the watchful eyes of the Order. "This is what you've done to us. You've killed this town," their eyes seemed to say, and I struggled not to believe them. My evenings concluded with cleaning the kitchens and bathrooms. By the time I was able to have a moment to myself, I was too exhausted to plot my return to Talia.

A month after I was forcibly returned, I was able to go back to the normal schedule, though I was constantly shadowed and forced to be accompanied on all the missions I went on. I managed to use the excuse of, "I need to use the bathroom" to slip away and warn the necromancer before my "companion" caught up to me. I'd take a finger and warn them that if I caught wind of them killing someone again, I'd take more than that. I hoped that they'd heed my warning, but I was prepared to come across them again and exact punishment. Soon though, my companions grew suspicious, and the best I could do was kill the necromancer quickly and painlessly. Each time we got wind of a new attack, I hoped that we wouldn't find Talia, and each attack was worse than the one before.

First, it was a single necromancer so doped up on Nectar his body continued to roll around on the ground after he was beheaded. The next attack was two necromancers, a young girl and boy, who destroyed an entire town except for a single baby that was brought into the care of the Order. I felt Niamh's eyes on me as I killed them, and I knew she looked for any hesitation that would be reported back to the Preceptor.

We got called out to Torrick, a small settlement outside of Braeton's city limits, and had cornered a necromancer. As we approached the necromancer, a short woman who looked to be in her early forties, she threw her hands in front of her, a piece of paper shaking in one.

"Wait! Please! I have to go to Braeton; I have a message to deliver."

That made us pull up short. Niamh stepped forward, forcing the necromancer against the wall of a stone building behind her. "Who could you possibly be giving a message to?"

"I was told to hand it to someone named Lysandra Spits, she works for the Order. Do you know her?"

Niamh turned to look at me so fast I was sure she'd break her neck in the process.

I shrugged, as confused as she was. She turned back to the necromancer. "No, we don't. But if you give us the message, I'm sure we can track her down." Niamh reached for the letter.

The necromancer shrank down to her knees. "No, I can't give it. If I don't hand it to Lysandra personally, Talia won't give me Nectar."

Again, Niamh's head turned towards me, and I swear I heard her neck snap. "Are you fucking kidding me?" She asked before knocking out the necromancer. "This thing clearly knows something that we don't. We're bringing it with us. You're going to be the one carrying it."

I slung the necromancer over my shoulders, surprised by how light she was, and we brought her back to the Order. Niamh threw our new captive into one of the infamous cells below the Order while I informed the Preceptor of the Order's newest resident. I watched as one of our teachers arrived with a smattering of grizzly-looking tools and a grim face. He entered the cell, and the door was locked behind him. Only the Preceptor on the outside of the cell had the key and would only unlock the door once the teacher inside knocked on the door. The screams began soon, telling me that the necromancer woke up and participated in "research" that would make Braekios proud.

"You don't need to be here," the Preceptor said to Niamh and me, and while Niamh shrugged and walked upstairs, I felt frozen to the spot.

"I know, but I need to know what's happening."

A chair was brought down for the Preceptor, and I leaned against the wall, certain that this was going to be a long night. The screams continued for most of the night, punctuated only by cries of, "I don't know anything!" Which was an obvious lie and led to even more terrified screams. The screams turned into sobs before I heard low murmuring and knew that we'd soon have the information we desperately sought. The teacher knocked on the door, and as he emerged, a crumpled bloody piece of paper in his hand, and I caught a glimpse of what remained of the necromancer. She was missing her fingernails and toes, blood streaming out of the ends, face beaten to the point of being unrecognizable except for the gold eyes that stared at me, beseeching me to help.

I gulped down a shaky breath and tried to keep a neutral face, but inside I shouted. We were supposed to be the good ones, the ones keeping the peace and ensuring that everyone was able to live the life they wanted. There was nothing monstrous about the look I got from the necromancer, but the aloof look on the teacher and the blood soaking all his clothes casted him as some kind of malevolent deity.

"Well?" The Preceptor asked and I turned, eager to look away.

"The letter didn't say much. Ostyx is amassing an army on an island called Syrenthia that lies due East of Hennix."

"Did she share how to get there?"

Mr. Rah shook his head. "I tried multiple times to get the info from her. She only said that it took four days to reach the coast."

"Do we know how many necromancers reside on the island?"

Another headshake. "No, but considering that we haven't heard of this island before, and Hennix hasn't had any recent necromantic attacks, it can't be too large of a population."

"It couldn't be easy," the Preceptor murmured, rubbing his forehead. "We need to attack that island, but to do that we must know exactly where it is. We can't afford wandering around in the ocean in hopes we come across it." We lapsed into silence as the Preceptor thought. After a few long minutes he said, "Reach out to the head of Hennix, we need to find out why an island that's apparently so close to us, has been unknown until now."

A raven was sent to Hennix and we quickly got a response. The Preceptor shared with us that the locals believed the island to be haunted, anyone who'd traveled near the island never returned, their boats slowly drifting back to the docks before being quickly burned to release the negative energy they held. They were all warned to never approach the island and raised generations to never acknowledge it.

Chasseurs gathered at the Order's headquarters here in Braeton, and soon the building bustled with activity. Rumors spread around the city about what could be going on as supplies were delivered in bulk. All classes were canceled due to the teachers and Preceptor spending all the days locked in a room discussing strategy. I made my own plans during that time, too, knowing that the only chance of getting that necromancer out of the cell would be on the day that everyone was outside the manor. I stole drying clothes from the lines outside, pocketed extra food after meals, and stole medicine from the sick bay when no one was looking. I couldn't find a backpack but did manage to find a sack used for potatoes and stuffed all the supplies into it.

One week after everyone descended on the Order and we found out about the island, we were finally pulled together and given orders by the Preceptor. "Our destination is the island Syrenthia, home to the Fae General Ostyx and his army. We don't know the exact number of necromancers who reside on this island but anticipate it to be around three hundred. We also have enough evidence to believe that humans are being held captive on the island. Our objectives are threefold: rescue the humans, kill the General who's responsible for the production of Nectar, and cull any necromancers we come across. We've communicated with the port of Hennix and they agreed to allow us to commission their boats for our use. We leave for Hennix in two hours, where you'll spend the night. Tomorrow morning, you'll depart for Syrenthia. Say goodbyes, gather your supplies and your mettle, because this will be a battle to be remembered."

The Preceptor left, the teachers trailing behind him and those gathered broke apart to talk and worry. I didn't need to share my fear with anyone else or have their nerves rub off on me, so I decided to take the day to walk around Braeton and take in the sights, potentially for the last time. Walking through the market square, I took in the smells and bought all my favorite snacks, not caring that I'd spent my entire purse.

I let my feet guide me and I found myself at a house I'd actively been avoiding since I learned the truth. I looked up at the large brick home and I saw the rich, purple velvet curtains that framed the windows. I walked up, past the perfectly shaped rose bushes, and my hand found its way to the door before I was able to stop myself. I knocked twice and a balding, blond man opened the door. I took him in, the gray dress coat and the perfectly tailored black dress pants doing nothing to hide the liver spots forming on his hands. I knew he dressed this elaborate, whether he had guests or not.

"Yes, can I help you?" The man with my chocolate eyes and straight nose said, taking in my wrinkled clothes and missing ear, the disgust in his expression almost completely hidden.

"Do you know who I am?" I asked, my voice shakier than I wanted it to be.

"Am I supposed to?" Did he not see it, or did he not care?

"It's me. Lysandra." His forehead wrinkled in confusion, and I felt my anger rise.

"I don't know a Lysandra."

"It's me, Dad. Your daughter, the one you sold to the Order so that I wouldn't interrupt your life."

His eyebrows shot up. He backed up to close the door, but I managed to wedge a foot in the doorway.

"Do you honestly not remember me?"

He shook his head. "No, of course I do."

"Why, Dad? Why did you give me away?" Angry tears fell.

"We couldn't parent you. You were a wild child, and we knew that you'd be happier somewhere else."

"I was a baby! You could've raised me, could've loved me, you chose not to! Now I'm off to fight and I might die, so that you and your wife can continue to pretend to be better than the rest of us."

The anger left me shaking and I let the man who sired me nudge my foot out and close the door. I sat down on the doorstep and sobbed, not caring that people looked my way and made snide comments. For the first time since I found out about how I joined the Order, I allowed myself to think about what my life could've been if I hadn't been given up. Maybe my parents would've grown to love me. Even ignoring me would've been better than abandoning me. If I was left alone, I could've still lived my life the way I wanted to. My skin could've been smooth and scar free, my ears could have stayed intact, and I could have had friends who didn't kill the love of my life. But that would never be, and I couldn't keep wallowing and wishing for something that will never happen.

I walked back up to the Order, taking the winding path past all the houses I grew so used to seeing, stopping at a caravan about to leave to pay for a barrel of wine to be delivered to Torrick, before heading to the roof of the Order, wanting to take in its breathtaking view one more time. As I opened the door, I saw Niamh sitting there and staring out over the roofs that puttered out little clouds of smoke. I sat down next to her and for a few minutes we were silent.

"You know, even though you chose those things over me, in the end, I'm glad we're going into this fight together." She leaned her head against my shoulder, and I let her, trying to imagine a future where we emerged from this alive.

The time to leave for Hennix grew near and Niamh left without me, as I stated that I "needed to use an actual bathroom one last time." The hallways were empty, and I crept into the Preceptor's room, looking through his desk for the key that went to the cells. Pocketing it, I grabbed the pack of supplies I'd put together and made my way into the basement. The necromancer looked worse since the last time I saw her, no more than a skeleton. She was so far gone that she didn't react to me approaching her, only lifting her hands after I unlocked her feet. "Thank you," she breathed into my ear. "I didn't want to die here."

We limped out of the cell and onto the road behind the building. In the chaos of the afternoon, no one noticed a chasseur pushing a cart with a large barrel down the road to where the caravan waited. If the driver noticed that I whispered, "Good luck, wait a few hours before you get out. Don't go back to Syrenthia, it's not going to be safe there soon," to that barrel, the caravan driver kept it to himself. I wished I could've helped more, but I couldn't risk discovery and being thrown into the cells myself.

I managed to return to the group of chasseurs as the Preceptor limped forward once again. "I have said all that has been needed. It's time for you to leave."

Wow, that was a shitty pep talk, and I heard a few others grumble about it, but we all shouldered our bags and began the walk. The Preceptor would stay behind, not only because of his age, but because he would be needed to teach future generations about this moment in history. When he did, how would he say my name? As a benediction, hoping that I'd pass on my wisdom to the new generation? Or would he say it full of spite, a warning to others about what would happen to you if you chose to go against the Order?

Chapter Sixteen — Lysandra

"I have witnessed them scream when in pain, but I do not believe they feel it, merely they believe they are expected to feel pain and act as if they understand its misery. Though necromancers have Fae blood giving them enhanced senses, their forms are entirely human. This means that they can bleed and die just as easily as humans. A blade to the throat, broken limbs, these will incapacitate a necromancer just as they would a human."

—Braekios Journal #13, page 4

We walked through the woods where most of us trained, and I looked at faces I both recognized and didn't. I saw scars on hard faces, and some missed pieces of themselves like me. We were survivors, perhaps we could survive this, too.

The march was quiet, and I chose to walk next to Niamh. Our hands reached out to touch each other occasionally, trying to reassure each other that we were still there. Hennix was quiet except for the gentle lapping of the waves. The Order managed to get the inn to loan us rooms. We were going to have to put four in each room, but it meant that we were going to be able to spend the night comfortably and out of the elements. The food was hearty, and the fire lit in the fireplace crackled merrily, easing some of the knots that formed in my body from the journey over here. I chose to sleep on the floor, letting Niamh and the other chasseur sleep on the bed.

In the morning, we ate breakfast and made our way to the beach, loading our gear up and getting a quick demonstration of how to steer the boats. We had a rough idea of how far the island was and the plan was to arrive late at night, using the darkness to hide our presence.

The boats were small, but sturdy. During the fall, the fishermen would often go on day-long fishing trips, hoping to catch enough to last their families through the winter. Each boat was equipped with a small cabin, large enough where we were able to sleep two people at a time if we didn't mind curling around each other. Shifts were created and we took turns steering the boat and resting. There was nothing to do except stare off into the horizon and my eyes would grow tired from straining to see Syrenthia in the distance. On the fifth and potentially last day, the sea turned against us. White foam formed on the waves, and we were thrown from side to side. The clear blue sky turned gray and dark clouds formed. Fat raindrops fell on us as we put on our rain gear.

The rain fell quick and fast, making it difficult to see anything except the little lantern that each boat had at its tip. I heard multiple people around me getting sick over the edge of the boat, and I fought my own urge to vomit. I sank deep into the killer's calm, imagining that I was on solid ground in front of my peaceful lake, and I felt my stomach settle, so I focused on making sure the sail stayed upright and pointed in the right direction.

There was a loud splash, followed by multiple screams, and I struggled to understand what happened. I peered into the darkness and managed to see the vague outline of a boat, capsized. I felt hands grab at our side and we swayed with the motion, close to tipping over. We pulled the person on board, and I recognized the drenched figure as Sylphie.

"It's okay, we got you." I whispered soothing words, trying to rub some warmth into her trembling form.

The rain stopped as we made it to the island, though with the fog and the darkness I couldn't make out anything beyond the trees. As the boats pulled in, I looked around and swallowed an unsteady breath. We started with fifteen boats, and only ten were beached on the sand. We'd lost five boats and our group looked much smaller, so it was clear that the people were lost with them. This was not entirely unsurprising. Since Braeton was landlocked, the Order didn't train its acolytes in swimming, but it was heartbreaking to see so many of us lost to the fickle waves. I tried not to get too frantic, but my heart raced as I looked for Niamh. I spotted her a little ways away, watching as people hugged and tried to regain some warmth.

"That was shit. Makes my list of the top ten worst experiences of my life," I said, siding up to her.

She looked and I saw relief in her eyes as she smiled. "I don't know. Do you remember when Sylphie got chicken pox and it spread around the dorm? We were all itching like crazy. I still have the scars. This was way better than that, easy eleventh place."

Mr. Rah and Ms. Emile, a stern woman in charge of the littles in the Order, motioned for us to gather. "It's time. While the necromancers sleep, we'll find this Ostyx and kill him. We'll go through the town together. We know that there are humans being kept somewhere on this island, and we'll rescue them if we can, but Ostyx and Nectar are our first priorities. We're racing against the sun and don't have the luxury of time. We got intel that there's a large manor at the top and we expect that is where we'll find the captives. At the manor, we'll divide into two groups. One, led by Emile, will go down to the lower levels and search for the captives. The other group, led by me, will go upstairs, with the objective of finding and killing Ostyx."

He listed off names and we divided ourselves up. I was assigned to Emile, and Niamh to Rah. After one last hug and whispered goodbye, we walked up the beach and through the silent trees. The town was silent, peacefully sleeping and we walked past making little noise. We were about to ascend to the manor when a cry of "Hey!" rang through.

We turned to see a drunk necromancer wobble out of a building that must've served as an inn, and as one of the chasseurs ran forward to kill him, the necromancer managed to let out a loud cry of "Intruders!" that echoed through the town. Quicker than we could respond, the town sprung to life. I watched as necromancers opened doors and a few strode out into the street, violence in their eyes.

"Kill them! Quickly!" Came the request from Rah, and the Order responded, pulling out weapons and pulling necromancers out into the street, killing them without hesitation.

My fellow chasseurs moved around me, but I couldn't do anything beyond stumble forward a few steps. Children were pulled out of embraces, still in pajamas, no doubt abruptly cut off from sleeping in their beds. Their shrill screams as they watched their guardians get cut down in front of them had me flinching, and the shrieks only ended when they were killed themselves.

"No!" I tried to grab Sylphie's hand, stopping her from cutting the throat of a young boy who cowered, and she glared at me as she shook me off.

I looked for Niamh and found her running after Rah, who decided to go on ahead, not bothering to get his hands bloody. Did they not care that they were killing potentially innocent people? We had no way of knowing if any of these necromancers were like Talia, unwilling to use their abilities, and now we'd never know. I ran to catch up to them, determined to end this quickly so that these people could live. I wasn't going to stand for this. I didn't know when or how, but I was going to hold the Order accountable.

"Where are we going?" I panted when I finally caught up.

Niamh turned, looking at me. "Rah's going after Ostyx. He's hoping that the mayhem in the town will lure him out from wherever he's hiding in the manor."

We kept running, up a large stone staircase to a manor that sat imposingly on the top of a hill. Niamh and Rah pulled the doors open, peering into the darkness beyond for any threat before we entered the house. Inside, they looked for a staircase leading up and they climbed one that circled up.

"Wait, shouldn't we look for the captives?"

Rah looked at me as if I was a child interrupting an adult conversation. "Ostyx is the bigger priority. The captives won't be safe if we can't ensure that Ostyx is out of the picture."

I had to try to convince him. Who knew what was happening to the captives while we looked for Ostyx? We needed to free them as soon as possible and point them in the direction of the boats. "We can look for a back way out once we find them and lead them to the beach. We don't need to engage Ostyx. The Order prioritizes human life. Who's to say that Ostyx won't use them as leverage against us if we don't get them out of here?"

Niamh hissed, "Lysandra, respect your elder."

At Rah's rage, I bowed slightly. "Forgive me Teacher. Would it be okay if I split from you? If we were to engage Ostyx in combat in a tight space, I may be in the way. I would like to free the captives and regroup with the rest of the chasseurs in the town."

Rah waved his hand dismissively. "Fine, go Lysandra. It's not like we could trust you not to side with Ostyx against us."

That stung, but I didn't let it deter me from lighting a torch and walking down the long staircase and into the dark hallway. It grew colder and soon I made out the occasional murmured word. I entered what I assumed was the dungeon and I moved quickly towards the voices I heard. At the first cell I reached, I saw a large group of humans grouped together in the back.

"What's going on?" One asked when they saw that there was someone outside the cell.

"The Order has arrived to free you. They're attacking the town and Ostyx, so now's the time to make a run for it," I whispered, using the light of my torch to examine the lock.

"Finally," was the response I got as the person walked closer.

I narrowed my eyes trying to make out any facial features and stopped as I realized who arrived at the bars. "Lucien?" I whispered, reaching through the bars towards him.

"Lys," he said, grasping my hand with fingers that were crooked from healing incorrectly. I had no doubt he got them from trying to pick the lock and getting beat for his attempt.

"What happened to you?" In the light, I saw the sharpness of his cheekbones, the sunken eyes and the ragged beard that took up most of his chin and throat.

"They got me on my last mission. We were attacked by a group, but instead of killing me, they brought me here. I thought it was to hold me for ransom against the Order, but when I saw the rest of the people here, I realized they had no intention of letting me go."

"I'm going to get you out," I said, raising my hatchet.

It took almost ten strikes, and I would need to resharpen my hatchet, but the lock fell to the ground, and I pulled open the heavy steel door.

"Do you know a way out of here?" I asked as the humans slowly filed out of the cell, cautious hope lighting their eyes. Lucien shook his head and I sighed, of course, it couldn't be easy. "All right, Lucien, take these people and go upstairs. When you get to the main floor, make sure there isn't anyone around and go out the front door. Follow the path down into town, the rest of the Order's there, and they can help you get to the beach where we're docked."

Lucien nodded and started to usher the group upstairs. "There's more, way more of us down here. Are there even enough boats?" He asked, before walking up the stairs.

I didn't say anything, knowing that there wasn't, but I was determined to get as many of these people home as I could. I worked my way down the row of cells, freeing more and more humans, until I finally reached the end.

I was about to turn around when a woman put a hand on my shoulder, stopping me. "I think there's someone in the next cell."

I cocked my head trying to hear the person in the next cell, but it was too dark and silent. I thanked her, gave the group the same instructions as the first, and went to the cell. I broke the lock open and walked in. Inside the cell was a large wooden table, with a form lying deathly still on it. I didn't expect the person to be alive, but I refused to leave another corpse down here for the necromancers to use. I approached and saw that the woman was breathing, barely. The hair was tangled and long, hiding the face inside it, but I didn't need to see the face to know who it was.

"Talia," I cried, sinking to my knees in front of her. She was barely more than a corpse, her form sickly and stretched tightly over bones. Her arms were bandaged, but I saw the blood staining them. I stood back up and cradled her head, pressing my forehead to hers. "Talia, I'm here. Please wake up. Please." I waited, hoping beyond hope that she heard me.

I felt her eyelashes flutter against my face and pulled back to look into the silver eyes I missed so badly.

"Lysandra?" She asked, placing a shaking hand to my cheek.

I held it close to me, kissing the wrist. "Yes, I'm here. Let's get you out of here."

She nodded and I picked her up, carrying her in my arms. We went upstairs and I was about to turn left towards the main doors before she stopped me. "No. We can't leave yet. He has Nectar, lots of it. It needs to be destroyed."

"Talia, please, we can come back—"

"No. We can't. We don't know if the Order would let us return, I'm not risking it staying with Ostyx."

I sighed, of course she was thinking about others instead of her own escape. "Fine. Do you know where it is?"

She pointed to the right, saying, "He brought me into a room down there."

I carried her down the hall, stopping at the fifth one on the right. I opened the door to a workroom immaculately clean, with shelves lining all the walls, jars of Nectar on each one.

"What now?" I asked, not wanting to go around and break each one.

"Do you see those stems in the corner?"

"Yes?" I responded, eyeing the small flower stems, tucked away in a corner along with some other herbs.

"Do you have a flint on you?"

"Yes."

"Good. Place one on each shelf and light them up. They're incredibly flammable when dried and I know he hasn't gotten fresh ones since I got here. But you'll need to move fast, they won't take very long to catch."

I gingerly placed her on the floor by the door, well outside the explosive range, and placed a stem on each of the shelves in the room. Preparing myself to move quickly, I struck the flint. As I made it to the door, I heard a loud bang and turned to see that the first shelf had caught and was lighting the next one. I scooped Talia up and briskly walked to the front door, eager to get out of this place. I pushed the door open with a loud creak and as I heard a low chuckle, I felt

Talia press herself against me, trying to put more distance between her and the only person I knew she feared.

"Where do you think you're taking her? Her blood belongs to me." I saw Ostyx, for it could only be him, walking down the steps, drenched in blood, and shaking some of it off his gloves.

I looked around for signs of Niamh or Rah, and when he saw my eyes dart around, he laughed again. "Are you looking for your colleagues? I can assure you; they're dead. I'd hoped for a decent fight, it's been ages since I've been able to use my powers. Unfortunately, I didn't even break a sweat."

Niamh was dead? I hoped she was with Dinah somewhere, warm and content, watching over me. I shifted Talia and pulled out my hatchet, knowing I didn't stand a chance against him, but hoping that I could buy enough time for Talia to run and meet up with the others at the beach.

"Run Talia. Leave me here and I'll meet up with you at the beach."

"No, I won't."

She was so stubborn, but I should've known she wouldn't back down. "Fine, stay behind me." I closed the front door and propped her against it, putting myself between her and Ostyx.

Ostyx smirked at me, and I taunted, "What are you going to do, Ostyx? There aren't any bodies nearby for you to call upon."

I felt the air around us grow cold and remembered one crucial fact.

"I don't need any corpses." His smirk turned into a predatory grin, and I watched as ice appeared in the shape of a dagger before falling into Ostyx's outstretched hand. Right, pure Fae meant elemental magic, not necromancy. This fight just became a lot harder.

Chapter Seventeen — Talia

"It is unknown how necromancers receive the call from the dead. One necromancer told me that it felt the dead as waves like that of an earthquake and would then channel them into their body. Another informed me that it could see the threads that belonged to the corpses and would weave them in with their own. It appears the methods of reanimation vary just as much as the original Fae's abilities did."

—Braekios Journal #1, page 87

Lys went still and I knew she was prepared to defend both of us against an unknowably powerful enemy. I wished that I could stand by her side, both fists raised and ready, but I wasn't going to be able to help as it took all my effort to not fall onto my side. My father broke the frozen dagger he held into multiple and raised his hand, releasing three of them in quick succession, aimed at our heads. Lys pulled up her hatchet, angled to deflect them, and while she was able to force two to the ground with a loud shatter, one scraped against her left shoulder. It tore open the fabric and skin beneath it. She winced, raising a hand to her shoulder, and I saw blood coat her hand as she pulled it back. After wiping the blood off on her pants, Lys rushed in, her brass knuckles in place on her right hand and her hatchet held offensively in her left. Though her footsteps were steady and sure, she'd need to end this fight soon before the blood loss caused her to stumble.

Ostyx raised his hands, and a wall of ice rose with a grinding sound. The wall crept skyward to defend my father, but Lys was quicker. The wall grew, quickly gaining height, and Lys used her momentum to plant a foot on the wall, launching herself into a jump. At its apex she was above Ostyx's head, and she angled for a blow. Gravity would make the strike deep, and I hoped this was the end. It was hard to see through the thick ice distorting my view of the two of them, but I was sure that Lys would've made contact if not for Ostyx raising an arm, encased in thick ice. The hatchet sunk deep into the ice, and Lys, still holding on to it, was thrown against the wall behind them before crumbling to the ground. A trail of blood followed her descent.

The ice wall evaporated almost as fast as it formed, and my father advanced towards me. I scrambled to push the door open, but my weight wasn't enough to make it budge. "Now Talia, let's get you back into your cell." He leered over me, and I already felt the cold stones below my butt, in the cell once more.

He reached for me, and I screamed. "No! Please, no, I can't go back!" Terrified of that dark and suffocating cell.

Behind him, Lys rose to her feet, unsteady but growing more confident with each inch she straightened her body up to. Ostyx clamped a cold hand around my wrist, turning to drag me away, as Lys stalked up and sliced it off, blood splashing across her face. Ostyx dropped me to cradle his wrist to his chest, hissing.

"You revolting piece of human trash," he said, rage turning his eyes into lava as he turned towards Lys, full of deadly intent.

She settled into a defensive pose as Ostyx summoned ice dagger after ice dagger. The air whistled as daggers whisked through the air, aimed at any part of Lys left undefended. Again, Lys tried to deflect with her hatchet, but the collision with the wall left her sluggish and each dagger that contacted her hatchet forced her to back up a step. Her back was against the wall, Ostyx approaching like an oncoming storm. This wasn't going to be the end. I couldn't let her die in front of my eyes, ending our story that had just begun. I cast my mind around, looking for anyone or anything that I could bring to her aid. I went deeper into my mind than I'd ever gone before, and the strain of throwing my consciousness so far from my body had my blood rushing to my head, leaving me shivering from the cold.

"Please," I whispered, hoping that I could find someone nearby, and I finally felt an answer.

There had to be some dead somewhere. Lucien said they'd died from lack of food, and I suspected that my father would choose to keep them preserved for the upcoming battle instead of burning the bodies. Deep in the manor, I finally felt them, far out of reach from most necromantic abilities, including mine if I wasn't in dire need of their help. I overrode their desire to sleep, forcing them to join me, and I felt my nose bleed, my head throbbing with the effort. Lys was still fighting, and losing, blood coursing down her legs and she stumbled in a puddle of her blood as she stepped forward to land a high kick aimed at his head but hitting his shoulder.

Slowly, a group of twenty humans, more skeletal than human, emerged into the hallway and I flicked a finger at Ostyx. "Kill him," I said vocally, not having the mental capacity to issue the order telepathically.

Ostyx swung at Lys with a sword of ice, and she leaned down, shifting her weight to her front foot before sweeping her hatchet in an upward movement, shattering the sword. I saw the wheels turning in her head, determined to pull her back foot up for a kick that would send him to his knees, but Ostyx created a wall of ice around her foot before it left the ground, and while she tried to pull free, it was obvious that wasn't going to happen. He advanced on her, a cruel smile on his face when my army finally reached him. They pulled him down, and I watched his head disappear, bolts of ice shooting up into the air, but missing their targets.

"Get off me!" Ostyx ripped at limbs, tearing fingers and arms off, but there were too many of them. He grunted, and I knew my army used their remaining fingers to dig into him, their teeth to pull out chunks of flesh. Ostyx's struggle slowed, and the ice bolts stopped flying. My army pulled back, and I looked upon my father's broken form. Blood made it difficult to see if he was truly dead or acting, so I approached cautiously. I placed my hand on his throat and when I didn't feel a pulse, I sighed. It was finally over.

I heard Lys chipping away at the ice, and felt her hand grip my shoulder. I looked up at her relieved but strained face and as she placed a kiss on my forehead, she whispered, "It's not over yet. We have the chance to make a real change here, to make life better for both humans and necromancers."

"What did you have in mind?"

"You're not going to like it." She was right, I didn't like the plan, but I recognized the need. "Do you think you can do it? I don't want it to be too much."

"I can do it. I have to do it."

"Good. When this is all over, we'll relax. We could even spend all day in bed, if you'd like."

"I'd like that."

"I'm not sure if you remember this, I don't know if you were conscious, but when we last saw each other I told you that I loved you."

Oh, so that dream I had was real. She blushed and stayed silent, waiting for my reply.

"You're everything good in my life, Lys, and I want you to stay by my side. I love you Lys, I think I have since I first saw you."

We kissed, slow at first, but growing passionate as our tongues intertwined. I reached up to tug at her hair affectionately, and when she groaned, I pressed up against her harder.

"As much as I want to continue this, we don't have the time." She was right, and I prepared myself for what was to come.

We reached the town, and I looked around me in horror. Bodies littered the ground, and while there were a few chasseurs dead, most were necromancers. I recognized the old man who sold hand-woven tapestries through a jacket of blood. He was on top of the corpse of a young boy, arm held out in defense. Both had wounds in their backs, and I could tell that they hadn't known where the attack came from. We had to step carefully and tried our best not to disturb the bodies quite yet. As we approached the door to my temporary home, I heard quiet sobs, followed by a shushing noise. Lys held out her hatchet and slowly opened the door, unsure of what lay behind. As she took a step inside, a snarling Rae lunged towards us, hands grabbing for her shirt.

The hatchet was raised to attack Rae but I sputtered, "Stop! Lys, Rae, back off!" Both turned to look at me, Rae's eyes going wide before letting go of Lys's shirt and stepping away.

I tried to rush forward only for it to be a slow stumble, but thankfully both women seemed reluctant to engage again. I finally reached them and placed a hand on each of their arms.

"It was you who betrayed us, wasn't it, Talia? To your precious humans, that's why you're not dead and everyone else is." Rae spat the words out at me, and I tried not to cringe away.

"It wasn't her fault, it was Ostyx's. We caught a necromancer who was sent to the mainland, and she told us everything." Lys holstered her hatchet and held my hand before telling Rae about the necromancer who she helped escape.

"Thanks, I guess. Not many of your kind would help a necromancer." Rae's eyes softened slightly though she remained tense.

"How did you escape?" I asked, noticing the group of seven children behind her, peering at us suspiciously.

"I was in the bar when I heard the attack happen. I snuck out the back and pulled whatever kids I found with me into your house since I knew it would be empty. I'm sorry, Talia, I didn't know that Ostyx would do that to you! I thought you'd get your hand slapped and that would be it." Rae started to cry, and I realized that she felt guilty for what happened to me.

"Don't blame yourself, you couldn't have known that would have happened. My father was a dick to everyone."

She looked up at the manor. "Was?"

"He's dead Rae. Almost all of us are. But we have a chance to make it better for those still alive."

She took a shuddering breath. "Tell me what I can do."

Between Rae and I, we raised all the bodies around and they walked obediently behind us. The kids wanted to help, too, but considering we were about to deal with the Order, we told them no. Slowly, we continued our way down to the beach.

Between reanimating the long dead back in the manor and raising the rest of the town here, the mental load grew to be too much, and walking became difficult. I relied on Lys, leaning on her shoulder and letting her guide me. The sound of the ocean waves grew louder until we finally arrived at the beach where the people gathered seemed to be separated into two groups. While all looked shell-shocked, it was clear who were the captives and who came with the Order. In the middle of the assembly, I saw Lucien arguing with a teacher from the Order as we approached the beach.

"The chasseurs deserve to go back first! We're more valuable and need to inform the Preceptor of what happened here." The teacher stomped her foot like a petulant child.

"No," Lucien said, not backing down from the glare thrown his way. "The chasseurs haven't spent months deprived of food. You came here to rescue them. They deserve to go back first."

"Who's to say that they'd send a boat back for us?

"Seeing as they probably don't know how to get back to the mainland, we'll send a chasseur, one," he hastened to say when the teacher opened her mouth to argue. "who will guide the group back. I'm sure the Order will come back for us. Unless you don't trust your fellow Order members?" The teacher's face turned a shade of scarlet that almost matched the blood stains on her torn jacket.

Lys cleared her throat, and both turned to see us, eyes going wide when they saw myself in Lys's embrace as well as the dead army behind me.

"Yeah, that isn't going to happen," Lys said. Rae and I moved our army into position, having them circle the remaining chasseurs, forcing the ones who tried to run to the ground.

"What are you doing?" The teacher asked as she pulled at the arms holding her.

"I'm making us better," Lys said, lowering me to the ground as my legs buckled and gave out.

"Glad to see you found her," Lucien said, nodding at Lys.

"She found me. Took me out of the darkness into the starry sky." I almost felt Lys blush.

Lucien smiled and I was surprised to see that it was genuine. Maybe the Order and necromancers could exist peacefully.

"What now, Lys?" Lucien asked, his stance relaxed despite being restrained.

Lys took a deep breath. "You're going to take these captives back. Lucien's right, Emile, they come first. But you'll bring this note to the Preceptor."

Lys walked forward and handed a scroll to Lucien who took it, asking, "What does it say?"

"It's informing the Preceptor that Talia and I are keeping chasseurs hostage." Cries of outrage rose from them, and they struggled harder. "They will remain hostages until the Preceptor comes here and signs the contract."

"Contract?"

"Yes, it gives all necromancers access to Philipa's Tincture, which the Order will be taught to make, and the ability to apply to the Order if they so wish, if they take the tincture. In return, the Order promises a just trial for all necromancers found guilty of a crime. We can be better; we must be better."

As I remained on the ground, letting the wind brush sand over my hands, Lys organized the return trip, with Lucien leading the captives back. When we could barely make out the boats on the horizon, we marched the chasseurs back into the cells.

Although they'd be locked up, they would have way better conditions than the original captives, making sure that all had light, food, and water. Lys and I took a bedroom and when Lys gently pulled out a vial of Philipa's Tincture from her bag, I almost wept. The pressure of having so many voices in my mind gave me a pounding headache that clouded my vision and made me weak. I took it, feeling instant relief as the bodies crumbled to the floor in a pile outside. We would light a pyre for them later, after a long and much needed nap.

We offered the tincture to Rae and the kids, but unsurprisingly, none wanted to take it and the deceased Rae raised were sent to clean up the town. Rae and the kids took up residency in a few of the rooms and tidied up the manor.

It only took a few days for the Preceptor to reach us, coming with two of Lys's other teachers. We argued, a lot, but after they saw the effect Philipa's Tincture had, and Lys's retelling of the choice Rah made to attack Ostyx first instead of rescuing the humans, the Preceptor relented to our demands. The contract was signed, and we organized the return of the chasseurs. I taught whoever wanted to learn how to make Philipa's Tincture, transforming the ruined workrooms into classrooms. The first few lessons were tense as I tried to convince the chasseurs that I wouldn't attack them, but soon I gained their respect as a knowledgeable teacher and the atmosphere turned academic. I even learned a few new techniques on replanting from a man who claimed he was the gardener for the Order.

I rarely saw the necromancer kids, who ran amok in the manor, setting up random traps to trip people and trying to prank Lys, but Rae was a constant shadow, standing outside the door to my classroom. I asked her once if she wanted to join, but when she scoffed and walked away, I decided not to push it.

Lys was busy coordinating with the Preceptor and teachers, writing and then rewriting the contract that would be sent to all the Order Preceptors. I rarely saw her during the day, and she frequently collapsed into our bed at night, grumbling about how difficult and stubborn the others were being.

Soon the day came for the chasseurs to return home, and we saw them off at the beach. There was a group that hung back, shifting from foot to foot, and I recognized them as the group that had been studying under me. After a brief discussion one of them broke off and approached us, and I wasn't surprised to see it was Lucien. Since being released he'd regained the color in his face, and the way the wind swept his hair seemed to suit him. One of the first things we did once the contract was signed was whittle a cane for him to use, and he no longer looked uncomfortable using it to walk.

Lys chuckled when we saw him turn from the group towards us, and I turned to her. "What's so funny?" I asked.

"I think I know what Lucien is going to ask us," she said, trying to repress the smile that graced her face.

"Oh? Do share," I said, elbowing her, watching Lucien limp over.

"No, I don't want to spoil the surprise."

"Spoilsport," I laughed, pinching her slightly. She grinned again and kissed the top of my head.

"Look at you, Lucien, you almost look like the version I used to know," Lys said as she went in to hug Lucien. He hugged her in return before giving my arm a friendly light squeeze.

"It's all thanks to you two. I'm not sure we would've been rescued if Talia hadn't done it, or if you hadn't stopped Niamh from killing that necromancer."

"I'm sure you would have broken free sooner or later," Lys said, waving off his comment. "Did you want to ask us something?" She asked with a wolfish grin.

Lucien blushed before clearing his throat and spoke. "Can we stay here? Not all of us, obviously some are already in the boats. But we," he gestured to the small group behind him, "really loved learning about the tincture and we want to learn more. You're such a great teacher, Talia," he rushed to say when he saw my raised eyebrows. "We know you can teach us more. We promise we'll behave and do whatever you say. There's so much more we can learn. Once we learn as much as we can, we'll return to the Order and teach everyone there, too! I know that the Preceptor and the rest of the group know how to make the tincture, but we could teach them so much more! Please, please say you'll let us stay."

I had no idea what to say, and turned to Lys, pleading in my wide eyes. Like all the times before, she knew what I wanted to say, without needing the words to say it, and she stuck her hand out to Lucien.

"Of course, Lucien. We welcome anyone, necromancer or human. We'll find you guys your own places in town."

He returned to the group, and we heard a loud cheer as he relayed the news. Slowly, the boats filled up, the Preceptor the last one to leave. "What will you do?" The Preceptor asked as we stood on the beach, watching the boats leave.

Lys leaned her head against my shoulder, and I nuzzled at her hair with my nose. She thought for a moment before finally responding. "We're going to stay here. Lucien and the others want to stay, why not see if necromancers and humans can get along? We're not far though, Preceptor, and we will come if we hear you aren't following the contract. We may be an island, but trust that we have our ways of staying up to date with the news."

The Preceptor paled and I couldn't tell if he was trembling because of the cold or because of Lys's threat. "You can be sure; I have no intention of going against what we've signed. Like you, Lysandra, I, too, want what's best for all who live. You two have proven we can exist with the necromancers. I believe it's time for a change. I suspect that I'll be able to convince the others of the good this contract can do. It will take many meetings, and I expect we'll need to call for a convocation. I'd like for them to hear first-hand experiences. Can I count on you to come when I call?"

Lys looked at me, and I nodded. She grinned. "Yes, Preceptor, we'll be there. Send a raven and we will come as quickly as we can." He was the last one to board the boat and we didn't watch them leave, returning to the manor to help clean it up and make it home. I never anticipated wanting to stay in the dreadful house, but after clearing it of the blood and airing it out it became brighter and more welcoming.

Chapter Eighteen — Lysandra

There were two rules we put into place for all who remained on Syrenthia. The first was to always show kindness to each other. This meant we accepted no ill word, or harm to each other. If this rule was broken the perpetrator was put into the cell for a time decided by their peers.

The second rule was to take part in a shared dinner. No matter where we were during the day, we were expected to return to the manor and help prepare the meal before sitting down at the table. The first nights were tense to say the least. The chasseurs and the necromancers were equally wary of each other, and Rae bristled any time one of the humans spoke with the kids. Conversation at the table was limited, usually between Lucien, Talia, and me, and while we tried to include Rae in the conversation she frequently chose to grunt or provide one-word responses.

The other chasseurs and I chose to continue our training, usually done in the courtyard behind the manor, and soon we had a peanut gallery any time we exercised. Their eyes were wide and while I desperately wanted to teach them, I didn't want to scare them away. I could tell that I wasn't the only one who saw their interest, and Lucien began to try and teach them. At his first approach they ran away, but upon returning the next day, they let Lucien give them each a branch and begin to teach them the basics of swordplay. Soon I was teaching them hand to hand combat as well as tracking, and one of the other chasseurs, Elaina, was teaching them how to throw knives.

Rae proved more difficult to teach than the others. I'd see her standing outside the door to Talia's work room, but any time I asked if she was going to join, she'd shake her head and walk away. It wasn't until I saw her flinch back from Sven who walked past her, that I remembered what Talia had shared about her life before Ostyx found her. That night I shared my thoughts with Talia, who grew pale as soon as I finished.

"You're right, that's got to be it," she said, before grabbing my hand and going to find Rae.

"They won't hurt you; you know," I said to her when we found her sitting on the beach alone that evening.

She buried her head in her arms. "You don't know that. They could be waiting for their opportunity."

"They've been alone with the kids plenty of times, if they wanted to kill them, they would have. What's really the problem?" Talia said gently, leaning her head against Rae's shoulder.

"I'm waiting for them to hurt me. Every time they move towards me, I can't help but feel as if I'm about to take my last breath."

Talia looked at me, and I knew she had felt the same way when we had first met. It seemed like ages ago and I knew she didn't feel that way about me anymore, but I still felt guilty over the way I treated her.

Talia pulled Rae in for a hug. "I felt the same way as you. I was certain that when I first met Lys, she was going to kill me. I was so certain that my anxiety practically killed me instead. But I choose to trust her, choose her to see me for who I am instead of what resides in my blood. You need to do the same, Rae. Give them a chance, they're good people. They wouldn't have chosen to stay here if they didn't see the good in us."

"I'll try," she whispered. The next time I saw her standing outside the door to the workroom, I caught her eye and cocked my head to the entrance. She took a deep breath and steeled herself before walking inside. I saw Lucien look at her from the corner of his eye, but he didn't do anything except to hand her an apron. He smiled slightly at her, and I saw her return with one of her own.

We experienced our first winter on the island, and I didn't miss spending time in the blustering wind or frigid rain and snow that plagued Braeton during that time of the year. Soon the weather grew warm, and then hot, humidity drenching us the second we walked out the door. We got word that a convocation of the Order Preceptors had been scheduled for the fall in Braeton, which meant we had a few months to prepare ourselves. Word had gotten around the mainland and we welcomed twenty-two more necromancers, and even a few humans. All were welcomed but were given the same rules. We rebuilt the town and slowly filled the houses. The street began to be full of laughter and song, and Talia reopened her clinic. We spent less and less time in the manor, choosing to be near the beach and away from the bad memories that still haunted the halls. It looked like we were staying here, at least for a while, and as long as it meant I was with Talia, I was okay with it. We decided to open a small school, tired of letting the necromancer kids run wild, and wanting to provide both them and the new human children a proper education. We let all who wanted to attend, which meant that we even had a few adults join us. Rae stepped up and decided to take on the role of instructor. It made sense for her to take on this role since she'd been the one to form such a close bond with the kids. The only subjects that she didn't teach was herbology, which Talia led when she was able to escape from the clinic, and history. After much discussion, it was decided that Rae would co-teach the subject with one of the chasseurs, and together they made sure to teach the prejudice necromancers experienced. Talia and I became something akin to local celebrities due to our part in the creation of New Syrenthia, and while the hero worship we received didn't really bug me that much, she began to wear a long-brimmed hat that hid her face. Everyone had a place here. Talia had her clinic, Rae her school, Lucien and the Other chasseurs spent most of their time between building new structures or going to the mainland for supplies and the occasional trip to the Order as our liaison. Everyone had a place here, except me. I floated around, taking time to help in the clinic or teaching combat and tracking to the students, but I didn't really have anything to call my own. As much as the convocation worried me, I looked forward to having something to do. I could tell that Talia knew and spent a lot of time trying to entertain me. We'd go down to the beach and have long talks, or we'd gather medicinal herbs around the island, but I saw the look in her eyes that spoke of wanting to be back in her clinic. I marked the date of the convocation in my calendar and marked off the days leading up to it. One week before it was time for us to leave, Talia pulled me down to the beach in time to see the sunset. We sat, her resting her back against my chest and her head leaning against me, as the sky lit up with golden hues of red, orange and yellow, and I felt that she longed to say something.

"Talia, is something wrong? You've been fidgeting way more than normal."

She sighed and shifted so that she could look at me. "This place is a dream come true for me. I never thought I'd be accepted for what I am, let alone be surrounded by people who loved me for it. "

"You made it impossible for us. How could we not love that big brain you have?" I tweaked her nose, and she swatted my hand away.

"Yet none of this would've been possible, if it weren't for you. You took a chance on me, Lys, and I'm so grateful you did."

"You took a chance on me too, Talia. Sure, it was more likely that your death would've been because of me, but you could've killed me the second you learned I was in your town."

"No, I couldn't have. I knew you were my chance at escape, and at a future I could only have dreamed of. Now look where I am. Sitting on a beautiful beach with the person I love most." She leaned up and I kissed her, savoring the way her lips tasted of windswept salt air.

She reached into her pocket and pulled out a small box. "Will you, Lysandra Spits, marry me and stay by my side as long as we both breathe?"

I gasped and choked on the air, sending me into a coughing fit. Talia patted me on the back until I was able to calm down and respond. "Of course, Talia, there's nowhere else I'd rather be."

She smiled and slid the silver ring inlaid with an emerald stone onto my finger. I intertwined our fingers and took in how good they looked together.

The long-awaited day came. The boats were loaded, and we said our goodbyes to Rae, Lucien and the others on the beach. The journey back to the mainland shouldn't be nearly as tumultuous as my first trip and I looked forward to finally sharing Braeton with Talia.

There would be challenges ahead, and I had no doubt that we'd struggle to convince the Order to work with necromancers instead of against them, but if Talia was by my side, I was invincible. Judging by the way she smiled and rubbed soothing circles into my hip, I could tell she felt the same way.

www.ingramcontent.com/pod-product-compliance
Lightning Source LLC
Chambersburg PA
CBHW070509300726
48975CB00007B/2384